A WORLD OF WEIRDITIES

Borgo Press Books by Ardath Mayhar

The Absolutely Perfect Horse: A Novel of East Texas (with Marylois Dunn)
The Body in the Swamp: A Washington Shipp Mystery [Wash Shipp #2]
Carrots and Miggle: A Novel of East Texas
The Clarrington Heritage: A Gothic Tale of Terror
Closely Knit in Scarlatt: A Novel of Suspense
Crazy Quilt: The Best Short Stories of Ardath Mayhar
Deadly Memoir: A Novel of Suspense
Death in the Square: A Washington Shipp Mystery [Wash Shipp #1]
The Door in the Hill: A Tale of the Turnipins
The Dropouts: A Tale of Growing Up in East Texas
Feud at Sweetwater Creek: A Novel of the Old West
The Fugitives: A Tale of Prehistoric Times
The Heirs of Three Oaks: A Novel of the Old West
High Mountain Winter: A Novel of the Old West
How the Gods Wove in Kyrannon: Tales of the Triple Moons
Hunters of the Plains: A Novel of Prehistoric America
Island in the Lake: A Novel of Native America
Khi to Freedom: A Science Fiction Novel
The Lintons of Skillet Bend: A Novel of East Texas
Lone Runner: A Novel of the Old West
Lords of the Triple Moons: A Science Fantasy Novel: Tales of the Triple Moons
Makra Choria: A Novel of High Fantasy
Medicine Dream: Being the Further Adventures of Burr Henderson
Messengers in White: A Science Fantasy Novel
Monkey Station: A Novel of the Future (Macaque Cycle #1; with Ron Fortier)
People of the Mesa: A Novel of Native America
A Planet Called Heaven: A Science Fiction Novel
Prescription for Danger: A Novel of the Old West
Reflections; & Journey to an Ending: Collected Poems
A Road of Stars: A Fantasy of Life, Death, Love, and Art
Runes of the Lyre: A Science Fantasy Novel
The Saga of Grittel Sundotha: A Science Fantasy Novel
The Seekers of Shar-Nuhn: Tales of the Triple Moons
Shock Treatment: An Account of Granary's War: A Science Fiction Novel
Slewfoot Sally and the Flying Mule: Tall Tales from Cotton County, Texas
Soul-Singer of Tyrnos: A Fantasy Novel
Strange Doin's in the Pine Hills: Stories of Fantasy and Mystery in East Texas
Strange View from a Skewed Orbit: Autobiographical Reminiscences
Through a Stone Wall: Lessons from Thirty Years of Writing
Timber Pirates: A Novel of East Texas (with Marylois Dunn)
Towers of the Earth: A Novel of Native America
Trail of the Seahawks: A Novel of the Future (Macaque Cycle #2; with R. Fortier)
The Tulpa: A Novel of Fantasy
Two-Moons and the Black Tower: A Novel of Fantasy
Vendetta: A Novel of the Old West
Warlock's Gift: Tales of the Triple Moons
The World Ends in Hickory Hollow: A Novel of the Future
A World of Weirdities: Tales to Shiver By

A WORLD OF WEIRDITIES

TALES TO SHIVER BY

by

Ardath Mayhar

THE BORGO PRESS

An Imprint of Wildside Press LLC

MMIX

CONTENTS

INTRODUCTION

Of all the people whom I've known—but never actually met in person—Ardath Mayhar stands at the top of a very small list of folks whom I'd really like to spend an afternoon with—just jawin' for a few hours about life, the universe, and everything, you understand, while sipping a cool lemonade and watching the interplay of emotion and shadow across that wise and gentle visage. I would find the experience so inherently pleasurable, I think, that I would sacrifice much indeed to attain that goal.

Alas and alack, that the particular universe in which we both abide has cruelly decided otherwise, for neither of us can travel very far any longer. So, while I can speak to my dear friend on my cell phone or via e-mail or through any of a variety of other conveyances, I can't actually share an ordinary tea with her—which is much my loss. She dwells in East Texas—a world of fancy entirely wrapt unto itself—and I inhabit a fantasy existence of quite another devising, that strange hodgepodge of culture, camp, and cruelty, SoCalifornia.

But the next best thing, perhaps, is to enjoy the flavor of her lovely mind and unusual sensibilities in quite another way—through the stories and novels that I've been reprinting and publishing under the Borgo Press Imprint of Wildside Press.

The worlds of Ardath's imagining are as diverse as the stars that sprinkle the night sky, filled with hues both dim and bright, characters who prance upon the stage with largess of life and intimations of death, and stories that twist and turn through byways and highways unexpected—each piece just a little different from anything you've ever encountered elsewhere.

Only a master fabulist can produce such magic on command—and this is one of the greats, no question.

One of the pleasures I've experienced during the three years that I've edited this line has been the discovery of good writers whom I'd never read previously. Now you would think that over a lifetime of voracious gobbling of texts—and I've pursued a love affair with words since I was four or five—I would have seen or heard of every pensmith worth his or her salt. Not so, gentle reader. We are each of us limited by time and life and the serendipitous chain of accident. I will go to my grave not having encountered dozens, hundreds, even thousands of authors whose works I would have treasured—if only I'd had the time to explore further.

Ardath is one of my great "finds." Her work is uniformly excellent, uniformly unique, uniformly unexpected. Her stories and novels are treasures to be savored. This new collection includes classic horror, regional fiction, vampire stories, traditional high fantasy, and tales that defy any attempt at even rough classification. They share a quality of writing and a quality of observation that most writers could not attain in a millennium of trying.

And they're *different*—different from *my* fiction, different from Stephen King's fiction, different from the fiction of any other author you'll ever encounter—anywhere.

I happen to think, in this particular instance at least, that *different* is good.

So, while my physical steps won't be heading in the direction of East Texas anytime soon, my soul will be there, oh yes, somewhere out in the piney woods and burbling swamps, where "the creek, it done riz."

And I know Ardath will be there too!

—Robert Reginald
San Bernardino, California
22 June 2008

What if Dracula had a cousin, who managed his disability more humanely than the Count did? He could be a lovable old gentleman!

THE VISITORS

Keeping a fusty old place like this in some kind of order has always been a terrible task. Even when I was young and vigorous, with help from the village available and money to pay for it, the effort taxed my energies. Now that I am old, it has become almost impossible.

The Master, bless him, can do nothing to help. Those in his state of health can hardly be expected to notice such matters as dust behind suits of armor. It is all I am able to do to keep the major chambers and the library cleared of cobweb and mildew, not to mention cleaning my kitchen.

Not that the Master eats much, nowadays. In his weakened state, he has given up even the pretense of an appetite. Yet I must feed myself and the occasional paying guests that provide our only income.

When those arrive, young Sonja comes from the village to help, bringing gossip and bits of newspaper and even, sometimes, a book to while away my solitary hours when Master and I are alone here. She is a dear girl, and I would like to see her travel, learn new ways. Here there are terrible traditions of superstition and bloodshed.

It was with great anticipation that I opened the letter from Master's solicitor, notifying us that a party of English visitors would arrive within the fortnight. Sir Hubert Lansdowne, his wife, their daughter Melissa, and three young ladies who were her schoolmates intended to stay for some weeks, if the accommodations suited and they found the country of interest.

At once, I struggled up twelve crumbling flights of stairs to set the red flag on its pole at the top of the highest tower, signaling the woodcutter to send his son to run an errand for me. Ulrik was a likely boy, always willing to help, in return for odd bits of pastry or such that I could spare from the kitchen. He would get word to Sonja, so that she could help me scour the guest rooms and the dining hall and put the music and sitting rooms into order.

Then I went to inform the Master. He was dozing, as usual, in the deep chair before the fire that burned day and night, year-round, to warm the chill of age from his bones. When I tapped, then opened the door, he looked up, his black eyes heavy with sleep.

"Dorina?" he asked, as if there could be anyone else who would enter his chambers so informally. Then his gaze sharpened. "You have news," he said. "I can always tell, for you turn rosy pink and your wrinkles disappear."

I chuckled in spite of myself, for Master has always been a great tease. He pretends that I was a raving beauty and the love of his life, back in the lost days when I was young and he was less ancient than he is now.

"Behave yourself," I said. "We are about to have guests again. Sir Hubert Lansdowne and party. Six in all, which should give us enough money to survive next winter with a bit left over. I have sent for Sonja. In twelve days, there will be company in the house again. Are you pleased?"

He had become so decrepit in late years that it was difficult for him to go down to meals with his guests. Still, he always seemed to enjoy hearing news from beyond our mountains, and he made an entertaining host. History was his passion, and those who, like our guests-to-be, came here to learn about the historical riches of this land found him a mine of information.

There really was no other reason why foreigners should put up with the drafts and crumbling splendors of this old pile, when they might enjoy the comforts of the great hotels in Belgrade.

Master had created a reputation for himself among those who recommended foreign junkets for their wealthy and titled friends. Never had there been a dissatisfied visitor, and most had written voluminously after returning home. Indeed, some kept up a regular correspondence with Master, valuing his friendship as much as his treasury of historical lore.

His face creased into a thousand wrinkles, and his dark eyes brightened. "Indeed, that is good news. I worry, Dorina, what is to become of you when I am gone. You have served me well all your life, as your mother did before you. I dislike the thought of leaving you destitute."

I shook my head. "Never fear, Sir. I save a bit of my wage, whenever you have the money to pay me. I spend almost nothing. There will be enough, no matter what happens."

Looking at him, I wondered how long he could last. All of the Torquilius family were extraordinarily long-lived, as was well known. Yet Lucius Torquilius had outlived even the most ancient of his predecessors. If my calculations, based upon the tales of my mother and grandmother, were correct, he would now be in his hundred and seventieth year. Surely even he could not hold onto life much longer.

I sighed. Imagining life without the Master, my work, and the castle was difficult. But I had work to do. "I must busy myself with the preparations," I told him. "You might be thinking of interesting places to suggest, suitable for young ladies who may not be capable of clambering about the mountains like those young men who last visited us."

I left him poring over a great book, locating sites of monasteries, battles, ruins and such. Why people were so set upon visiting such mournful relics I had never understood, but I was happy that they did. Otherwise we might well have starved.

With Sonja's and Ulrik's help, by the time the party arrived the state chambers, the guest rooms, even the corridors in the guest wing were shining clean. We could not prevent stone from crumbling, mortar from dropping from ancient crevices, but we could sweep up all traces of dissolution and whitewash the worst areas of damp and decay. Which we did.

When the carriage drew up outside the great doors, I was ready, Sonja beside me, Ulrik just behind her. With three of us to do the work, I knew we could make these newcomers comfortable.

In the lower reaches of the kitchen, savory scents rose from bubbling pots and sputtering spits. It was a joy to have the money for real cookery!

I curtsied, and Sonja copied my movements. Ulrik jerked his awkward bow as the Englishman descended from the vehicle and helped down a fragile creature a-billow with crinolines and curls. Amid all the pale pink finery I glimpsed a sallow little face wearing a fixed smile, like that of a corpse.

Shocked, I hurried to help her up the steps, leaving Sonja and the boy to greet the young ladies and help the coachman and footman with the luggage. "Let me take you to your room, Madame," I said. "Surely you are exhausted from your journey!"

She glanced up at me, her pale face ghastly. I could feel her arm tremble as I took it and supported her up the steps. "Thank you. I should like...that." she whispered. "But my husband might...be angry."

"Nonsense! I shall explain that you needed rest. I have handled gentlemen before this, be sure of that. One who can serve the Torquilius is able to deal with any sort or image of mankind, believe me."

She sank onto her bed with a grateful sigh, and I pulled the draperies (mended, but so carefully the darns did not show) to darken the room. She turned so that I could loosen her clothing, and once that was done her eyes closed.

"Thank you...."

"Dorina," I supplied. "At your service, Madame."

"Thank you, Dorina. I am so very weary. Tell my husband that I shall certainly be down for dinner. Or before."

"I shall send Sonja up to unpack for you, if you like," I said. "But if you would rather sleep, she will do that while you are downstairs, later."

"That would be best...," and she was asleep.

When I returned to the entry hall, Sir Hubert was far from pleased. He was berating the footman for some lapse when I appeared, and he turned to me. I saw at once that he was one of those, new to wealth, who felt it their obligation to be rude to those who served them.

"Where is my wife? Florence is never here when I need her!" His bulldog face was scarlet.

I stood silent until he calmed enough to listen. Then I said, "Mrs. Lansdowne has gone to her rooms, Sir, to rest from the journey, as is proper. She asked me to tell you that she will be down before dinner."

My instinct was not wrong. More than once we had entertained these new "nobles" from England. Their fortunes came from coal and railroads and industry, the newspapers said. They aped their titled associates, but a few years of affluence could not instill in them either good manners or an appreciation for culture.

I sighed internally. This was not going to be one who corresponded with Master afterward. But he was our guest, and I nodded to Sonja, now shepherding the four young ladies toward the branching stairway.

"If you will come with me, Sir Hubert, I will take you to the Master. He is very old and avoids the stair except to come down to dinner with guests. But he would like to greet you, as usual, in his study." Behind us, as we spoke, evening had arrived, and the lamps of the coach shone red as the vehicle rattled away.

All my life I had lived among the nobility. I had learned how to deal with inferiors, of whatever kind, and now the Englishman seemed a bit quieter. He nodded and followed me up the stair, where we took the left branch, leaving the young women to chatter away up the right to their wing of the castle.

Master's deep voice bade us enter. I stepped aside and said, "Sir Hubert, Master. When he is ready to go to his rooms, ring the bell and I shall return to show him the way."

"Thank you, Dorina." Master turned his dark gaze upon the Englishman, and Lansdowne seemed to deflate. Even his square jowl drooped under that brilliant scrutiny. But as I closed the door, I could see him take his seat in the chair drawn up beside Master's.

I had no time to dwell upon our new guests now. Dinner must be completed and set through the serving slot between the pantry and the long sideboard. Without a staff, we could not serve formally, but the food would be fine enough to silence any criticism.

When I peeped through the serving slot, I could see those new-comers spaced along the table, with Master sitting at its head, the Lansdownes on his right. Sonja, tidy in her neat black dress and white apron, indicated the buffet. There was a moment of silence, and then Mrs. Lansdowne stood in a rustle of skirts and began serving herself. Her husband came as well, his face a bit paler than usual, his expression more thoughtful than I had yet seen it.

The girls followed her briskly, and I smiled. Young appetites were a joy to cook for! As they passed along the buffet, I replenished dishes that emptied, pushed forward any condiment or item that was not readily within reach, and observed them closely.

The first of them had to be the daughter of the family. Her square face and pugnacious jaw reflected that of her father almost too faithfully. No beauty, she had a certain air that attracted me. Something of her mother was there, though I could not quite tell what it might be. A homely and dependable girl, I judged her to be.

The next was slight, fair, fluttery, a typical English miss, without anything to distinguish her from any other. Almost too lacking in personality. Phyllis was a suitable name for someone so light-weight. I found her somehow disturbing.

After her came the small dark girl they called Julia, whose brown eyes caught the flicker of motion as I pushed forward a dish of preserved apples. She looked at me and smiled, and I warmed to her. Not many of those her age ever noticed people who served them.

The last was a surprise. Teresa was a redhead, tall and slender. Her motions were languid, and I wondered why she was attracted to this lively crew, for she seemed uninterested in anything, from food to the company. Even after she sat and began to eat, I watched her.

She took no part in the conversation around the table, and when asked any question, she simply shrugged and ignored it. As the four misses sat together on one side of the table, it became obvious that Teresa wished herself anyplace except where she was. I noted that Master was watching her closely, a furrow of concern between his thick eyebrows.

Why had she come if she cared nothing for this journey? I puzzled over that as I waited to set the dessert out onto the buffet. Even when all had finished their meal and moved into the drawing room, I kept wondering. At last I went to bed, after checking that each of the guests had everything needed for the night, with questions still buzzing in my head.

* * * * * * *

We were so remote from the nearest farms and the village that quiet was a way of life at the castle. Though sometimes wolves howled in the distance or owls mourned in the ancient trees of the forest, the nights were restful. That night I woke suddenly, my ears ringing with some sound lost in the transition from sleep to wakefulness. When I sat, I realized the slight breeze that had whispered around the castle for the past day and night had died away. Stillness enfolded the darkness, but into the midst of that came another shrill cry.

It sounded like a small child.

I wrapped my cloak around me and hurried into the corridor. From time to time the sound came again, and I kept my senses focused, taking my directions from the whimpers and small screams reaching my ears. Down I went, until I was in the old sculleries, distant from the more modern kitchens the Master had made for me. Something rustled in the darkness, and I wished I had brought a candle. Though I knew every twist and turn of the corridors and stairs in the great house, I could not see in the dark.

As I felt the wall, making my way toward the hiccupping sobs that now racked the invisible child, something whisked past me in the blackness. A whiff of scent, delicate but spicy—was that the Master's cologne? It was not the same...much too sweet! A trailing edge of cloth touched my cheek, and then whoever it had been was gone.

Still fumbling through darkness, I felt my way forward until I touched a warm bundle. It shrieked in terror, and I knew I had come in time. Who or what had brought a frightened child into the Master's house?

"Shh...shhh," I breathed. "It is only Dorina, come to take you to the fire and the light. I am not going to harm you." I took up the small shape and stumbled back, finding my way by instinct as much as anything else to the warm kitchen, where the hearth fire still held red coals.

The little one shivered convulsively in my arms, but I set it in the chair beside the hearth while I stirred the coals and added more fuel. By the flames that flickered to life, I could see a round face, big blue eyes, a little nightcap, a blue blanket wrapped about the small body.

I knew her! "Nadia!" I said. "Small Nadia, it is only I. Where is your mother?"

She whimpered, being still too young to talk clearly, and I took her into my lap and sat by the fire, warming her, reassuring her, while I wondered how she came there. Then I shivered. There were old tales of missing children, taken by terrible beings who drank their blood. Not in living history had anything of the sort occurred, and I'd doubted they ever had. Yet what had brought a farmer's child over the miles she certainly could not cross by herself, into the house of Torquilius?

When the fire was burning well, I unwrapped Nadia and examined her closely. There was a small cut beneath her left ear. A drop of blood had dried just below it. Again I shivered. The old tales had told of the Wampyr's mark, and it had been much like this.

Who?

I knew the tales gossips told about Master. Anyone as old as he, living an isolated life with few servants, often was held to be one of the dread ones. I had heard such tales of others too, all of whom were now dead. Master was the only suitable candidate left, and Sonja carefully did not tell me the gossip she heard concerning him.

Yet I had lived for all my life in the same house with him, finding him always civil and sometimes even affectionate and teasing. It could not be Master, whatever the tales might be.

The child fell asleep, exhausted with its own fright. I laid it again in the deep chair and sought out the small room delegated to Ulrik when he came to help me with guests. It took some effort to rouse the boy, for he slept deeply. When I explained the errand he must do, he looked fearful for a moment.

"Through the forest in the dark?" he asked. "And carrying a child? Ma'am Dorina, I am afraid!"

I held up the candle I had brought and looked down into his tanned face. "I will send Master's pistol with you," I said. "Once you reach your father's cottage, he will go with you to the Gerlach farm to take the child home, and you will feel quite safe with him at your side."

I stared into his wide eyes. "But say nothing to our guests about this. We cannot drive them away with tales of strange things happening. There will be silver coins for you and your father, once they pay us, if nothing happens to frighten them."

I arranged a sort of sling, into which I set the sleeping child. It hung over the boy's shoulder and back, leaving his hands free to hold pistol and lantern. I watched until the bobbing light disappeared into the forest, and then I turned to the stair, my legs aching with weariness and stress.

Though I wanted with all my heart to return to my bed and pull the covers over my head, I knew I must tell the Master about this. He must know what was happening in his house.

I did not tap at the study door but unlocked it with the key from my jangling bunch. Beyond the study was his small library, and beyond that again his bedroom. I tapped at that door, but I could hear no harsh breathing. He slept quietly, for such an old man.

"Master!" I pushed open the door and stepped into the room, where a small lamp burned on a table beside the window. "Master, I must talk with you!"

For a moment I stared at the curtained bed. No thin ridge marked his presence there when I pushed back the drapery, and I turned to look elsewhere.

"Dorina?" His voice came from the corner where he had arranged a cushioned chair and footstool for nights when congestion made it difficult to sleep in his bed. He motioned for me to sit on the smaller chair at one side, and I dropped into it gratefully. "Something has happened?" he asked, almost as if he had expected that.

"It has. I heard a cry from below, about two hours ago, I think. I flew down, lightless, to find what it might be, and in the old scullery there was a very small child, young Nadia Gerlach, from the second farm this side of the village. There was a...mark...on her neck. A drop of blood...." My voice trailed off, as I thought with horror what that discovery might mean. Only now had I settled enough to realize all the ramifications of my discovery. The old villains of the tales had taken children to satisfy their unnatural appetites.

Master's eyes gleamed in the lamplight. For a moment his lips thinned, and I saw the outlines of his canines through the stretched skin. He knew, none better, what this might mean. Yet it was not he who had done this, I knew with all possible conviction.

A long howl from lower on the mountain interrupted the night. Master turned his head sharply, and for a moment I saw the young man he must have been, keen, alert, dangerous. When he looked back at me, his gaze was filled with sadness.

"My ancestors did terrible things, Dorina. When I was young, I also did things that make me cringe to think of them. But I relinquished those habits, renounced my heritage of blood and terror. I did not take the child, my friend."

I nodded. "I knew that. And, knowing it, my question is, who beneath this roof is guilty of the act? What was your opinion of Sir Hubert? Could he be one of that...fraternity?"

He looked down at his clasped hands, almost transparent now with age and self denial. "No. He is a small man, clever in one single way. He can create wealth for himself, though he has no conception of doing it for others. There is no possibility that he might be one of the Wampyr."

"Then what of his wife? She is a strange one, though terribly frail for such work," I said.

"There was no taint in her that I felt. Their daughter, too, seemed too much of the earth, practical and prosy, to share that dread heritage."

"Then it must be one of the young ladies. Which? How did you judge them?"

He leaned back in his chair and closed his eyes. His voice was a murmur. "The silly one, Phyllis, hardly exists as a person, I think, though she giggles infernally. Yet there is something troubling about her, though I cannot identify exactly what it may be."

That had been my impression, too.

"The dark child, Julia, is very human, very charming. She talks little, but what she says makes good sense. I should hate to think she could deceive me about such a matter, yet who knows what lies in the heart of anyone?"

"What of the third, Teresa?" I asked. "She strikes me as strangely alien to the others. She seems to take no interest in her companions or anything around her."

He nodded slowly. "Teresa. She puzzles me, as well. But she is bloodless, languid, without strength. That might, of course, be for lack of...nourishment. She stirred the food on her plate, but she ate nothing. I notice such things." His tone was dry, and I knew he had perfected such deceptions before my grandmother was born.

He sat straight and held out his hand. "Dorina, it is two hours before dawn. If anyone here has unnatural tastes and was prevented from satisfying them with the child, he or she may be remedying that lack at this moment. Go and check on the rooms. Every one of them, Lansdowne and all. I am not infallible."

I touched his cold fingers and turned to that task.

* * * * * * *

The corridors were chilly and damp. All the torches we had left burning in our wing had guttered out, except for one or two. Those gave little light as I hurried in my felt slippers. Up the stair into the other wing I sped, finding the corridor lit with the fine wax candles we saved for use when guests came. Those would burn all night, and even now they had a good two inches left.

The first door opened into the rooms occupied by the Lansdownes. Those opened into a mutual dressing closet, and the first should be occupied by Florence. She was in her bed, visible by the light of the dim red lamp left burning for our guests.

Through the closet, I moved toward the other room; before I arrived I could hear Sir Hubert snoring. Those two were obviously not hungry. Besides, I had watched them chew and swallow. Why had I not looked more closely at the habits of the girls? But I had been busy with serving.

I slipped out again, across the corridor to the door of the room where Melissa Lansdowne should be asleep. She was, her wide mouth open, her square jaw ugly in the dim light.

I sighed and went forward. Next was the chamber I had allotted to Teresa. The door opened silently, for I always eased the locks with an oiled feather before new guests came, for screeching metal is annoying. The door swung inward, but no light shone inside the big square room.

I caught a candle from the sconce beside the door and moved into the darkness, pushing a circle of light before me. Something crouched in the middle of the bed, white-robed, its eyes shining green, like those of a wolf.

As it rose from its crouch, I backed toward the candelabra on the marble-topped table and touched flame to eight candles. They flared into life; then I saw streaks of blood trailing down the front of a lawn nightgown, whose bottom edge touched the limp shape of the girl Teresa.

Her eyes were open, but they saw nothing...and then I was too occupied to notice anything else, for the girl on the bed sprang toward me, a feral snarl distorting her bloody mouth. Phyllis!

I gave a cry of warning and terror as I lifted the heavy silver candelabrum and dashed the flame toward those wide blank eyes. Phyllis howled, dropping to all-fours and dabbing at her face as if her hands had turned to paws.

I backed from the room, to find Mrs. Lansdowne behind me. To my astonishment, she held a pistol, primed and ready for use. Her thin hand was steady when she pushed past me.

"What danger?" she asked. Without waiting, she moved into the room I had just left.

That fragile woman could never deal with a Wampyr! I went after her and caught at her shoulder just as she fired point-blank into the creature's face. The load hit Phyllis squarely, but she was not dead. Still she quivered, trying to rise, trying to see her prey through blinded eyes.

Even as I watched, her terrible wounds began closing. I dashed back into the hallway and took down the heavy silver crucifix from the niche in the corridor. Staggering, I returned to that dreadful room, to find Phyllis almost on her feet again and Florence Lansdowne on her knees behind the sofa, praying.

Without pausing to think, I swung the crucifix. Phyllis, turning to meet the noise of my approach, seemed to sense its movement, but she was too slow. The silver arm of the cross crunched into her skull, and her shriek rang like a knell through the ancient halls.

She crumpled to the floor. The nightgown, now patterned with blossoms of blood, went flat, flatter, as the body beneath it dwindled to nothing.

I caught my breath with a sob. Then I turned to the bed and its pitiful tenant. Teresa had good reason for her languid movements and lackluster ways. How long had this errant Wampyr fed upon her, undetected, unsuspected, while the party traveled?

A curse and a thud caused me to turn. In the doorway stood Sir Hubert, looking bewildered. "I say!" he bellowed. "What is happening here? Florence, what have you done?"

There came another step, feeble and halting, from the corridor. Master appeared in the doorway, his cane trembling in his hand.

"I suspect," he said gently, "that she has saved the lives of my housekeeper and your young friend Teresa. This poor mad girl...."— He gestured toward the anonymous heap on the floor—"was obviously attacking her."

I turned again to the moaning girl. Her throat was punctured, two neat holes that still dribbled dark blood. But I knew, because I had lived all my life with the legends, that she would live and heal, now that her attacker was dead. There would be no more of that kind created by the creature I had seen as Phyllis.

"We must get a doctor," I said. "But I wonder if you want the true tale of this night rumored abroad. Your daughter's friend was a dangerous companion."

Florence rose from her knees. The pistol was still in one hand, and she offered it gingerly to her husband, who looked down at it, up at her, and then at the injured girl. "What—what?" he stammered.

"Phyllis, dear," his wife said. "She went mad and tried to kill Teresa and Dorina and then me. I shot her. Then Dorina struck her with that crucifix on the floor beside her. Not a pretty tale to follow our daughter all her days, I think. She died of a fever, don't you agree?"

Then I understood. With all his bluster, Lansdowne had little confidence in himself, beyond the area of his business dealings. In his life, he followed the lead of this frail creature. She was by no means the helpless female she pretended to be.

An interesting situation. I looked up into Master's eyes and saw him begin to smile. He looked younger, less feeble than I had seen him in a long while.

Excitement, too, can nourish a Wampyr.

There are more kinds of vampirism than that which feeds on blood. Some batten upon emotion....

CHILLY WELCOME HOME

The snow made Carlyle look like a Christmas card. Norma turned off the state road onto the skimpy main street and thought with some amusement that the place had never looked so charming when she'd lived at home with Aunt Leigh and Uncle Forrest.

To her surprise, only one house was decorated for Christmas; the Collins place sported a neat evergreen wreath on the front door and a huge scarlet bow on the brass knocker. Old Mr. Collins was getting feisty in his eighties, she thought. He'd never had a good word for anyone or anything that she knew about, when she was a girl growing up in the neighborhood.

But the tall Victorian house where her grandfather had reared his family was now before her. Unlike the Collins house, it seemed dingy, the paint peeling, the shutter on the right-hand set of bow windows hanging from a single hinge.

It didn't look at all like the house where she had spent twenty years of her life. Was there a money problem? Surely her aunt and uncle would have let her know if they needed anything. She had a good job, a generous salary, and they knew she would be more than happy—grateful, even—for the chance to repay some of the kindness they had lavished on their orphaned niece.

She hadn't called ahead, knowing that the two expected her for Christmas Day, without any doubt or need for communication. But when she moved cautiously up to the side door, taking care not to slip on the icy flagstones, there was no light in the kitchen. She sniffed. Surely the rich smells of baking cookies, turkey, and dressing should be filling the air this late on Christmas morning. The icy roads had delayed her and she was at least three hours later than she usually arrived on her Christmas visit.

The door was locked. Carlyle was probably the only place left on earth where you didn't have to lock your doors or your car. Norma felt a chill along her backbone as she rang the bell her grandfather had put into place for the use of delivery people.

The jangle sounded inside, seeming to echo through emptiness. She'd never used it before or even heard it ring, for the days of home delivery were long over when she had lived in the house.

Again she pushed the button, hearing the lonely sound inside. What could have happened to her aunt and uncle? Unless one had had a heart attack or something equally desperate, they would be there. They would come at once, hurrying down the long double flight of stairs from the bedroom story or up the narrow steps from the basement.

Her heart fluttered with dismay and concern. She knew she had to get into the house, for she could see the car in the garage, when she peered through the dusty pane into the single space meant for a carriage. Thoughts of defective furnaces, buildups of carbon monoxide filled her mind.

She dug frantically in her purse. She had kept the key to the big front door, seldom opened, on her key ring for the past five years, more as a good luck token than anything else. Now she fumbled it in numb fingers and slogged through the flawless snow to the front of the house, glad that she had indulged in such sentiment.

When the door opened, after a hard push, she stepped into the front hall, always immaculate, always smelling of lemon oil and good cooking. Dust lay everywhere. There was no feel of life in the house at all—it loomed around her, as empty as an abandoned seashell.

"Aunt Leigh!" she called, her voice sounding odd and the echoes bouncing back at her from the lofty stairwell. "Uncle Forrest! Are you here?"

When the echoes stopped, there was still no reply. She was about to lift the telephone, which was also dusty on its narrow stand beneath the staircase, when she heard something. A footstep tapped on the uncarpeted landing above her head.

She backed out of the cramped cubby and stepped back to look up the stair. A shadow moved there, and even as her heart tried to stop with terror she realized it was only her aunt.

"Aunt Leigh!" She hurried up the first few steps, but the forbidding shape stopped her in her tracks. It was, indeed, her aunt, but strangely altered since last fall. Instead of the plump, cheerful woman Norma had known, this was a gaunt, gray, bitter woman.

Only her beaky Stanford nose and the black eyes remained of the aunt who had loved her all her life.

Norma stepped back in shock, almost losing her balance on the round braided rug beneath the bottom step. As she stood, speechless, her aunt descended the stair to stand face to face.

"Go away," her aunt said. "You are not wanted here." Then Leigh Stanton Morrison turned and began plodding up the steps again, her leaden feet so unlike the lively ones Norma had known that the young woman began to cry.

From above, in the shadows of the upper floor, came a voice that might have been her Uncle Forrest's. "Go away now!" it urged her. "Right away. And never come back."

Bewildered, Norma turned and pulled open the heavy door. Beyond it, the snow glittered in brilliant sunlight, and the street of quaint homes seemed normal and welcoming. Yet, when she stood on the veranda and stared up and down, she noticed that no smoke rose from chimneys that were always cleaned for festive Christmas fires. No bustle of cars and arrivals troubled the drives of any home she could see.

"I've got to find out...." She turned blindly toward her car and stumbled over a lawnmower, forgotten and buried in the snow. What was happening here? Her people never left tools outside in winter!

The car started easily and she backed into the street. Nothing was moving within sight, except for a single curl of smoke rising from the Collins chimney. Why was that the only home that seemed alive? Old man Collins was eighty if he was a day, and he never in his life had been neighborly or interested in celebrating anything at all.

On impulse, she pulled into his unshoveled drive. The wheels spun, but Norma disregarded that. Under his *porte-cochère*, she stopped and leaned on her horn. She blew it again, but there was no face at the long window, no hand at the door.

This was too much! She got out and ran up the three steps to pound on the painted panels. "You come out, Mr. Collins! I know you're in there! I want to know what has happened to my people and everybody else in Carlyle."

She ignored the silence of the house. Unlike her people's home, this one felt inhabited. "I know you're in there, and I'm going to bang on this door until you come. You'd just as well give up now as later." Her fist hammered loudly.

Beyond the door there came a soft step. The lock clicked and the door opened a crack. To Norma's astonishment, it was not the wattled face of Henry Collins that peered out at her. Instead, a soft, rosy countenance stared up into hers.

"I am afraid I don't know you, my dear," came a quavery voice. "Who are you?"

"Norma Stanton," she said, her tone sharp. "The niece of Leigh and Forrest Morrison, up the street. You do know them, I should think."

"Oh. Come in. Come in, my dear child. Of course I know your people. They used to be so sweet, when I first came to town and bought this house. But they seem to have been ill recently. I haven't seen them in weeks."

"You didn't go and check on them?" For some reason the conversation was making Norma very, very uneasy.

"I'm not pushy," came the gentle reply. "For one so recently arrived in town to pry into the lives of others—that is not a very nice thing to do, do you think?"

Suddenly, the girl was exhausted. Her knees trembled, and she felt as if she might sit on the floor. "May I sit down?" she asked, her voice almost as trembly as that of the old woman.

The woman clicked her tongue. "Of course, I should have seen that you're not well. Pale and shaky—why, you're sick yourself, poor child. Come into the kitchen and let me make you a cup of nice hot tea."

That was the last thing Norma wanted, but for some reason she found herself unable to say no to this sweet little old lady. She followed numbly, sat in the cushioned Boston rocker, and accepted the Minton teacup without protest.

Even as she sipped the brew, she wondered what she was doing here. "What is your name?" she managed to ask between sips.

"Lucille Avery Worsham. I bought this house when Mr. Collins died last summer. I must admit that I was welcomed nicely, but everyone seems to have found me wanting." She laughed timidly. "They now seem to be ignoring me. I thought I had found a friendly small town where I could be a sort of grandmother's helper, but I suppose that sort of place doesn't exist any longer." Her bright blue eyes brimmed with tears, but she brushed them away with the corner of a linen handkerchief.

The warmth of the tea made Norma's thick coat feel entirely too heavy. She shrugged out of it, letting it drop behind her over the back of the rocker. She felt a dew of perspiration form on her upper lip, and she set the fragile Minton carefully onto the small table beside her.

"I'm so sorry." She felt as if she had lost all her energy, her will to live. Even her concern for her aunt and uncle was subsiding beneath a wave of depression that threatened to submerge her entirely.

But Lucille Avery Worsham was even rosier than before, her eyes sparkling with energy, her small figure bursting with health and vigor. She bustled about, getting more tea, setting out a plate of cookies decorated with silver shot and colored sprinkles.

"I do love to have company at Christmas. Since my family went away, I don't seem to have any. Eat a cookie, do. And then we might go back to your family's house and see what's going on with them." The old woman leaned forward, her face close to Norma's, every wrinkle filled with concern.

They went together, walking up the snowy sidewalk in their high boots. At the walk, Norma paused, feeling almost unable to go forward, but Mrs. Worsham took her elbow and pushed her with gentle persistence.

"Come now. You are all worried, and surely there is nothing to concern you. We'll just pop in and make sure they're all right."

Norma didn't knock. She hadn't locked the door behind her, and now Mrs. Worsham pushed it open, for the girl felt unable to raise her hand. Walking forward was hard enough.

Together they went into the front hallway. "Mrs. Morrison?" the little lady called. "Do come down, Mrs. Morrison. Your niece is so worried about you!"

The steps sounded reluctant, but they came, two sets of them. Side by side, Aunt Leigh and Uncle Forrest descended the stair and stood before their tiny neighbor like children prepared for a scolding.

"You sent her away! Naughty people! What we need in Carlyle is nice young blood, energy, plenty of spunk. And you just turned away your own flesh and blood as if she were a stranger. Shame on you!" Her tone was playful, but the blue eyes had faded to a chilly shade.

Norma found the energy to look up at her aunt. The despair she found in those lifeless eyes filled her with terror, but already it was too late. She found herself exhausted, beyond the possibility of rest or recovery. With leaden feet, she moved to stand beside her people.

"Now that's much better," said Lucille Avery Worsham. "I do like to have my neighbors all together and friendly. You just have a nice Christmas visit together. And it would be lovely if your niece decided to stay on. Carlyle needs young people." She turned back and closed the heavy door carefully behind her.

Norma heard the clunk of the lock. With awful clarity she understood the reason for the deathlike stillness she had noted in the town. All energy, all will, all life was concentrating itself in the Collins house, in the round rosy person of that small woman, who was even now tripping through the snow toward her warm, Christmas decorated house.

She understood, but it was too late. Norma no longer cared.

No matter who you may be—or when—it is best not to kick a cat.

THE MAN WHO KICKED THE CAT

Ta-Neter sighed with relief, as the last of the basalt blocks trundled away under the supervision of the Pharaoh's overseer of building. The demanding task of securing the blocks and shepherding them down the Nile had been profitable, but the long trip was both dangerous and uninteresting. He had devoted five years of his life to the task. He prayed to all the gods that he would never be required to repeat it.

Gathering together his tablets of wax and clay, his case of styli, and the records of all transactions, he entrusted them to his servant to deliver to the overseers of accounts. Then, relieved of his cares, he set out along the sun-baked streets of Bubastis to discover entertainment fit for one as deprived as he.

He drew in his white robe to keep it from brushing against the sweaty and bare-chested laborers who thronged the street. One such as he held himself above them, for his parents had sacrificed much to apprentice him to a respected scribe. Now his smooth fingers and plump body attested to their wisdom. His quick mind and diligent nature had sent him farther along his way to affluence than his people could have guessed might be possible.

Ta-Neter could feel the fat pouch jingling against his thigh, secured by a cord to his waist. Various young women along the way cast longing gazes at his person, which told him they, too, heard the clink of gold. But these women on the common street were worn and coarse. He desired more silken-smooth fare, after such a harsh journey.

Now the fiery sun was low, and shadow was stretching across the street, cast by the low mud-brick houses along the way. Ahead lay the vast complex of the Temple, with random dwellings and merchants' stalls huddled against its imposing wall. To the right a wider thoroughfare opened, and he could see villas with gardens along its route.

Turning into it, he looked about. A woman stood in a doorway on his left, her gaze inviting. Ta-Neter slowed his pace, smiling inwardly at the sure instinct that led him here, which was clearly a quarter tenanted by high-class prostitutes. But the street was long, and he passed this first prize, feeling the first cooler breath of evening drift against his neck.

Now he saw that almost every window held a face, its eyes darkened with kohl, the framing wig carefully arranged. Gazing so, he stumbled over something in his path.

With a yowl, a sinuous black shape leaped beneath his feet and stood glaring at him, its feline lips drawn into a snarl. The impatience generated by that endless journey surged in the scribe. With a curse, he stepped forward and kicked hard, sending the creature thudding against a wall.

The cat fled, shrieking, into the shadows. Ta-Neter laughed, his voice echoing eerily between high walls on either side of the street.

Two shapes waited ahead, both clad in white, as he was. The flesh showing above the narrow linen skirts was dark—ebony-dark. The effect was intriguing, exotic, and he hurried forward to look upon them from nearby. His breath almost stopped in his throat when one turned and looked back at him.

She had a beauty unlike any he had found in his own kind. Her long neck, proud narrow head, glistening black skin gave her the look of a Nubian queen. He felt suddenly awkward, but he jingled his pouch suggestively. Her dark eyes gleamed, and her wide mouth curved in a smile.

Her companion, wordless, turned also to look. She was in every way the twin of the first, even to the golden pectoral about her neck and shoulders. Together, they surveyed Ta-Neter, who was by now panting with excitement. The women nodded in unison and held out their hands, one her right, the other her left. Ta-Neter, between and behind them, felt as if he were led like a child as they moved along the street.

Though he would have liked to walk between them, in time he realized that his position, slightly behind, was even better. He could watch the sinuous motions of their narrow hips beneath the white linen. He could follow the lovely curves of neck and bosom as they turned to speak with each other or to pause and look back at him. He found himself more and more intrigued, as the two turned aside to mount the ramp leading into a gateway.

He could see a villa beyond the gateway, but it was only a small part of the compound behind the wall. A pool made a long vista, flanked by tamarisk and myrtle. At its end stood a temple, not large but with proportions designed by an expert; the sculptures about it were exquisite.

The shape of Bast loomed, half hidden in the growing darkness, beyond the wide doorway.

The women turned aside from the main path leading to the temple and led Ta-Neter into the pillared entry hall. There a porphyry lamp burned, its gleam showing him other guests who had come before him. Three men spoke with three women in the chamber, but his guides did not pause.

They led him through into a central chamber, where a bright lamp burned in the place where a winter brazier would have filled the raised hearth. Beyond, on the platform with its covering of fine rugs, two more women waited.

Ta-Neter felt his breath come short. These were even more exotic than the Nubians. He had never seen their like, for their skin was white as alabaster, and their hair shone with a silvery sheen in the lamplight.

What god of good luck had led him to this spot? He sighed, unconsciously releasing the breath he had held on beholding the new pair.

The dark women drew him aside into a smaller chamber, where the platform was lower, graced with cushions and neck-rests of fine stuffs. The Nubians, still moving as one, drew away his robe, while the pale women entered, untied the cord from his waist, smiling, and set the pouch aside.

Something inside him almost protested, but Ta-Neter was too entranced to speak. Instead, he allowed the Nubians to lead him to the platform and assist him to lie on its soft coverings. As he watched, they removed their narrow skirts and their golden pectorals and stepped up beside him.

He closed his eyes in anguished anticipation. Something touched his throat, pricked quickly, and was gone. Darkness overtook him before his fogged mind could question.

*   *   *   *   *   *   *

He woke to flickering light on a painted ceiling. The cat-head of Bast gazed down, inscrutably, from her pedestal above him. The dark stone of the statue shone in the dim light, almost as had the dark flesh of the two Nubians. He sighed and looked about him.

Two sets of black eyes gazed back at him, seeming almost as inscrutable as the eyes of the goddess. He started, tried to sit, and found himself bound, lying upon a low shelf of stone set into the base of the statue. His heart gave a thump, and he croaked, "Help me!"

The naked black shapes moved, one to either side of the shelf. They began to dance in the half-light, sinuous as serpents—or cats. As his eyes strained, the shapes grew hazy and changed. He clenched his eyelids shut, then looked again.

Two cats stood over him, large as humans, black as death. Now those eyes glowed green in the smoky light of the lamp.

"Help me!" roared Ta-Neter, hoping the fair twins might hear.

Two white cats came through the doorway and looked down. One held a black cat against her breast. Its leg hung limp, and it mewed softly.

"See, Sister, he lies here helpless. None may abuse our kind here in Bubastis without paying a price."

The cat said, "Miw!" in an imperative tone.

A chorus of purrs filled the room, and Ta-Neter gasped a prayer to Amon-Ra, closing his eyes for the last time. A clawed hand touched his throat. He felt the steely tips gash his skin and a trickle of his own blood touched his neck. A rough tongue lapped at his skin.

His quivering spirit fled at last, knowing it would find no home and no faithful family to feed it in the afterlife. He would die, indeed, and come no more.

In some ways he was fortunate. He never knew what they did to his body thereafter.

Many years ago there was a news story about a group of students who were hiking in the mountains. They went into an old mine, whose tunnel ran straight into a cliff for almost a mile, and there were lighted candles along both sides, all burned down to the same length. How could one person light two mile of candles simultaneously? Of course that had to become a story!

THE MINE

The moon was big in the smoky sky, dim as a pewter dish. The fires on the Mountain glared brighter by far than it could, and the red light seemed to reflect off the grimy face of the satellite, making the Lady in the Moon look as if she needed a good wash-up.

Darrel didn't care, though. He could see, and that was all he wanted. He could find the dry-as-tinder spots where the tops of pine trees had fallen in storms and left the needles to wait for him. He could light his Never-Fail, Foolproof lighter, watching the yellow flame waver in the wind.

When each new fire caught, pine needles glowing red and then gold, flaring up to catch the dry branches and the pulpy trunks, Darrel smiled bigger and broader. This was the night he'd waited for since he was a tad. The night when he would get back at the whole of the Mountain clan who had never recognized his special qualities. The entire village would be trapped in the narrow, wooded valley, and Sarah Freeling, too, feeling so brash in her witchy power, secure in her house set on a knob of rock above the trail leading upward.

The pine cones turned into red-gold ornaments, there in the heart of the last fire, and he left them to crackle and spit their sparks far and wide. The village would burn tonight, and Darrel Gillen Weeks would laugh tomorrow.

Sarah would come to him. She'd have to. Without the villagers to barter for her handmade shirts and her willow-woven baskets, her bitter potions and her love-spells, she could never live up there, holding herself so high.

He set his feet into the track leading up the Mountain. He had left this for last, wanting to be safe from the flames he had set from south to north, from west to east in the centuries-deep mulch of the forest. Only this strip of woods running up the face of the height was still dark against the smoke of the sky, where the sickly moon peered through.

There was the old working where his family had taken out silver, in the very old days. Yonder was another, where the Freelings had dug as well, using the scanty metal to buy what they needed when one or the other went out of the mountains to the world beyond. But these were the shallow holes, scratched like animal burrows into the dark guts of the Mountain. Higher up, near the mountaintop, ran the long shaft, going for a mile straight into the side of the height like some huge corridor, the floor flat and packed with thousands of passing feet and barrows.

That was where he would take Sarah, when he was ready. There he would break her to his will. When he was done, they would come back out into the light of tomorrow, and they would be alone in the valley, together at last, and the rest of the clan would be scattered over the rim of the circling ridges and peaks, those that weren't blackened corpses in the ashes. He knew none would ever come back, for what would be left?

He chuckled, keeping time to the crunch of his boots on the trail. It was his night, his time. No one but the moon knew he was abroad, though he could hear the shouts and the clanging of metal on metal that brought out men to fight the fires. They could battle as they liked. He knew the Mountain, and he knew the winds, and he knew how to set traps of flame for anyone trying to stop his blazes.

Come tomorrow, he and his chosen woman would be the only living people left. He had decreed that, and the great surge of certainty he had felt all day told him that he was right. Cash Alter would be gone, with his gifts of flowers and wild honey. Jeremiah Crews would be gone, with his calf eyes and his mooning ways. There would be nobody left to woo Sarah Freeling except Darrel Gillen, and she would have to pay mind to him, once he stood alone.

The wind rushed upward, channeled by the hot breaths of the many fires. Smoke wreathed round his head, and he coughed, but it was his own smoke, and he didn't mind it.

The sighing of the living needles of the trees overhead was almost a whistle, and he whistled to match them as he trudged upward toward Sarah's lone house, safe on its bald knob from any spark that might blow the fire to the woods beyond it. She would be there. He knew it!

But when he came to the fork marking the trail that went to her dooryard, he found himself strangely reluctant to follow it. Not yet. This was his night. Getting Sarah would blunt its edge, take away the savor of his victory. He wanted to look down on that burning valley from the very top of the Mountain, to see the frantic people packing their shabby goods and scampering away up the granite cut leading out. The old cars and the old horses and the even older mules would go, taking with them all the ones he hated.

There would be no more laughter. His family might be poor, where once it had been rich, but tomorrow he would be the master of everything left, burned or whole, in all of Silver Valley. And of Sarah, who scorned those of Weeks blood and ways.

The track was steeper, now. His breath came harder than it had, but he was getting to the top. The shaft that ran, arrow-straight, into the hillside was near—there! The dark mouth was a perfect arch against the pale stone.

He turned his head to peer into the blackness. But it wasn't dark; a long double line of twinkles led off into the depths. Flames. But how could they get inside the mine, when the forest outside its mouth was still unkindled?

He stepped into the arch and stood staring down the perfect perspective of two rows of white candles, standing ruler-straight, rod-perfect, their shapes dwindling smaller and smaller until those at the farther end of the shaft blurred together into twin lines of yellow flame. He moved forward, trying to see how so many had been lit and had burned just to the same level.

An army of men had to have been there, every one lighting a pair of candles on either side of that lane of light. But the wicks were just burnt down to the wax—if such an army had stood there, armed with matches or lighters, how had they left? He had been at the mouth of the tunnel, and not a living soul had passed him! It reeked of...witchcraft? He shivered, then laughed harshly.

He found that he had been holding his breath and exhaled, the breath making the nearest flames tremble in the still air inside the Mountain.

Had someone gone the other way, deeper into the shaft? Darrel almost ran between the glowing lines, toward the point where they melded into one in the distance. But always they parted again, as he drew near, and never was there a glimpse of a human being to explain the strange phenomenon.

The air was hot, now, with the heat of thousands of candles. The smell of hot wax and burning wicks was strong and tickled his nose, and he stopped to sneeze. When he took down his hands, he found that he could see something at the very end of the double row. A pale shape, sitting on a shelf of stone.

He slowed his pace, drawing near with caution. Someone who could do this was unchancy, at best, and perhaps, at worst, dangerous.

But when he came up close enough to see, it was only Sarah, sitting there in her washed-out cotton dress and her ragged apron, waiting for him. That was a disappointment. He had looked forward to beating her into submission, dragging her here by force, subduing her after a delicious struggle.

"Sarah!" he said, stopping at the end of the lane of light. "What are you doing here?"

Something about her flame-lit face reminded him of the raddled disk of the moon, where the Lady was red-lit and sorrowful looking. There was an expression to her that he had never seen before. Not the patience that had accompanied her loss of parents and land (her witching had surely not prevented that!); not the sadness that she showed on the night she struck him in the temple and freed herself of his embrace.

Now she looked weary and sick, yet her slight body seemed surrounded by an aura of strength that he had never noticed before.

"Sarah?" he quavered again, his voice going weak and tentative.

She stood. Sarah pointed with one finger down the line of candles, and that to his right was quenched instantly, leaving a single strand to light the tunnel. They glittered in her eyes, which seemed multifaceted now, glinting with sparkles of their own.

"You have burnt the Mountain," she said, her tone soft and deadly. "You have not listened to me or to anyone, and you have scorned those who would have helped you. Now you must pay for your wickedness, Darrel; now you must learn what it is to suffer and to fear. I tried to help you. My parents tried to as well, and it was you, I know now, who threw them down the Mountain to their deaths. I see that in your wicked heart."

He almost feared her. But then he remembered—he was large and strong, and she, for all her courage, was small and slender. What could she do against him? He would conquer her yet!

"I have carried the name of witch all my life, but never have I used any of the terrible secrets I learned from my people. I have helped rather than hurt, healed rather than injured. But now I will use those deadly secrets. You have earned that, Darrel!"

She pointed again, her finger seeming overlong in the yellow light. The line of remaining candles flickered and began going out, one by one, beginning in the distance and moving swiftly toward the spot where he stood. The shaft grew dimmer and dimmer, and he turned and began to run back toward the entrance.

Her voice echoed in the shaft, pursuing him as he ran. "Your feet will tangle. You will find the hidden ways and workings that no man remembers. You will walk the deeps this night, Darrel Gillen Weeks, and you will learn Fear!"

The smoke and the night combined to hide the faint glimmer of lighter space that should mark the mouth of the tunnel, as the last of the candles died. He dashed himself into a knee of cut stone. Picking himself up, he fled onward, but now he was disoriented, and he battered himself from boulder to boulder, trying to find a way free of the cluttered edge, back into the trodden central aisle.

Again and again, he found himself downed. Blood was warm on his face, crawling down his back, his arms, into his staring and blinded eyes. He thought he was running in circles, but he knew that was impossible.

"I am in a long tunnel," he shouted. "I can't run in circles. I must come to the arch at last!"

The words echoed back and back and back, bouncing from unsuspected depths, niches, and lateral tunnels—the maze of workings that had been dug into the heart of the Mountain. There was no way to know where to run, what to use as a guideline, how to find his way out again.

"Daylight," he panted. "When the sun rises, I can see the entry. Then I can get out into the clean air again."

But when the sun rose, he was wandering in the gut of the Mountain, lost beyond finding, even by Sarah herself.

Before he learned Death, he did, indeed, learn Fear.

We did not invent evil, though, sad to say, we have added ruffles and flourishes to the original notion.

COME OUT OF THE SHADOWS, MY SON

Khalid's frail shoulders drooped beneath the weight of torches and tools, but his father kept adding things until all the equipment was loaded onto the boy. Before, Khalid's brothers had shared the burden; his father himself never carried the tools of his trade. That would not be fitting.

Khalid's mother touched his cheek with a work-hardened hand, and the boy tried to smile. When they were gone about the night's business she would weep, worrying all the while they were gone. She knew the dangers, for two of her sons had already been lost to the family profession.

Achmet glared at his son and his wife. "Enough delay. The moon is rising, and we must reach the tomb before the light grows stronger. Do your work, Woman. We will return at dawn."

He went out into the dimness before moonrise, and Khalid followed, silent and subdued. They crossed the stony patch before their doorway and went toward the site of the night's work. A distant grandsire had built his sandstone house very near the Valley of the Kings, for theirs was the most ancient profession. Now the family had dwindled to two males, Achmet and his son, who were the last of their grave robbing line.

The desert lay silver-gray on black, the shadows of the boulders through which they picked their way seeming as deep as caverns. Khalid shivered, for the breeze that whispered across the sand was chilly. He blamed that for his clammy hands and the quiver in his backbone, but he knew that was not the cause.

His brothers had gone into the black hole in the cliff that his father had located when he rolled away a sandstone block. Khalid had heard their voices, excited, then wary—and he had heard their cries.

He had begged Father to go to their rescue, to use the wickedly curved blade that had been his many-times-great-grandfather's, but Achmet stood silent, undisturbed by the shrieks of his children. He had not even flinched; he had not moved to help them.

Khalid, terrified though he was, had run a short distance into the tunnel, calling out to his brothers. But by then the cries had died away, and at the angle in the tunnel a slab of worked stone barred his way. No sign of his brothers had been visible, only the enigmatic seal that had strange characters carved on its face in hieroglyphs.

When he returned, sobbing, to his father, he gasped, "There is no reason ever to come here again. They are gone, and the tunnel is sealed. The entrance to the tomb is blocked—it would take many men to move that slab."

Achmet's eyes had glimmered in the moonlight. "We will return," he told Khalid. "You will go down into the tomb and bring out the treasures that must be there."

That had been the first time Khalid ever saw the madness behind his father's black eyes, but he had known better than to protest. Still, as they turned back toward the house where the mother waited, he had thought he might run away to the city. Other boys, younger than he, managed to beg or to work enough to earn a living. Anything, even starvation, would be better than what might wait beyond that seal.

Now, a month later, following Achmet again to the tomb, he thought of the symbols cut into the stone. Three flags in a row, something that looked like an owl, a great eye with symbols around it, an ibis. Many things he almost understood were there; as he went forward, he felt those symbols to be warnings aimed at him.

As if reading his thoughts, Achmet said, "The old gods are gone...dust blowing across the desert, lost in the wind. Have no fear of them, for this is a world where men fly through the air and cross the sands without camels. Men control the world now. I see you quaking, boy. Has the Imam not taught you of the Prophet of Allah?"

Khalid said nothing.

Achmet went on, "I have felt you thinking about running away to the city, starving and scrambling among the small rats of the streets. Ours is not a family of beggars! We are tomb robbers, bearers of an ancient tradition. We humble the mighty; we redress the balance of the world between the needs of the living and the desires of the dead."

The cliff was in sight, silvered at the top by the rising moon. Khalid drew a ragged breath, feeling his skin crimp into goose-pimples. Now it was his turn. It seemed that, having lost two sons, Achmet was determined to rid himself of the last. Khalid had no hope that his father would relent.

The boulder rolled away under their joint efforts. It was beginning to wear a mark into the stone beneath it, and Achmet examined it in the light of the newly kindled torch.

"We must hide this," he said. "It is our discovery. No other family should harvest its treasures. We will do that when you report what you find inside. Now in with you!"

Khalid had shed his burdens, and now he fastened a bunch or torches to the rope at his waist. He tucked a pry bar and a trowel and a knife into it as well. Then he turned to his father, his lips open to plead, but he saw no pity there.

The boy straightened his thin shoulders and moved to the black opening. How many thousands of years had it been since the sandstone boulder had sealed it away? What noble mummy was entombed there? What scorpions and spiders and vipers had bred there, undisturbed, for so many centuries?

Terrified, he crawled into the blackness. Yet he found he was more afraid of his father, now, than of the unknown before him. Holding the torch ahead of him, he moved forward, jumping when sand slithered or pebbles rattled beneath his foot.

Just ahead was the bend. But when he turned it, the slab was no longer there. He would not need his heavy tools, at least. Then relief turned to terror. What had moved that great slab, solid as the bed rock itself? Many men, explosives even, would have been required to budge it. But there had been no sign that any foot had stepped near the tomb since his brothers disappeared into it.

Khalid realized he was whimpering, deep in his throat. Staring into the gloom beyond the bend, he tried to push his torch forward without following too closely behind it.

"Mahomet?" he called, his voice quivering as he called his elder brother's name. "Are you there?" Then he froze, for there came a groan, a strangled gasp, as if someone badly injured had tried to respond.

He forgot his fear. If his brother lived, he must have help! Khalid moved forward as quickly as he could. Passing the bend, he found himself in a much larger space, where he stopped and raised his torch.

This was a rectangular chamber, with walls covered with hieroglyphics and figures pictured in red and ochre. One, a woman painted much larger than the shapes behind her, sat in a chair, holding sheaves of grain, the leash of a cheetah, and a cat that sat beside her foot, its tail curled about its hidden paws.

Khalid felt that her one visible eye was fixed upon him. She seemed to see him as truly as he saw her. He shook himself and lowered the torch to search for his brothers.

There was a shadow in a corner beyond baskets filled with ancient grain. That spilled as he pushed them aside to reach the still shape.

That was, indeed, Mahomet, but it was clear he had not stirred or groaned. He was dead, his eyeballs fixed, his lips pulled back in a grimace of pain or fear. Khalid felt for his heart, but it was a foolish gesture. He had already begun to dry into a mummy.

Khalid straightened the flaccid limbs. In his brother's hand there was a scrap of material. Khalid held it to the light: soft, pale. A thread of gold was woven into it, as if it came from the garment of a wealthy lady. He tucked it into his rope belt and turned.

His brother Hamet must still be here. "Hamet? Are you here? Call out, if you hear me!"

Discordant echoes rolled and rumbled about the boy, and he almost thought he heard laughter mixed into the noise. He calmed himself by an act of will.

"The old gods are gone," he said aloud. "Only the Prophet and Allah exist. I am not afraid." Even as he said it, he knew he lied. Something in his blood and bones knew there were things in this tomb that had strength and potency beyond any he knew.

"Hamet!" he shouted again.

He searched the chamber, but no other man-shaped shadow was there. He approached another, this one low and square. As he bent to enter it, he felt or heard or intuited something moving nearby.

Eyes watched him. Something approached. He held the torch low to scan the dusty floor. Twin sparks reflected its glare amid coils that marked the dust. A cobra reared its swaying hood on a thick body.

But Khalid knew cobras. He killed this one with an expert blow from his pry bar. Then he stepped over the squirming body and went into a much larger chamber still. The tomb chamber, he realized. This had been a woman of wealth but little importance, for no attempt had been made to hide the entrance to this place where her sarcophagus lay.

Glints of gold caught the light of his torch, but he did not heed them. He stared down at the body of his brother, lying atop the stone sarcophagus, its limbs arranged carefully, the face composed. No cobra bite had caused his death, Khalid knew.

He lit a new torch and set it in a bracket. One by one he lit others, until the chamber was illuminated. Gold was there, and onyx and jade and gems of many shapes and hues. A statue of Anubis stood in a corner, guarding a chest of ornaments.

As Khalid stared about him, he felt a vibration in the soles of his feet. Dust filled the air, and he heard the grumble of stone on stone. He darted for the doorway, ran through the other chambers and into the tunnel.

The slab was again in place, barring the entrance.

Khalid sank onto the floor and covered his eyes. Even if he shouted, he knew his father could not hear him. If he heard he would not help. Now he was entombed with his brothers, the dead cobra, and the nameless one in the sarcophagus.

Would the slab rise again? Did some counterweight lift it, after a set span of time?

Khalid doubted that. This was a trap, and all the sons of Achmet were caught in it. How long had it waited to spring, and for what purpose had it been set?

For a long while he sat shaking, as a torch in the farther chamber began to burn out. He extinguished all but one...to die in the dark was terrible, he felt. If he could make them last until thirst or bad air killed him, that would ease his dying.

He thought of his mother, now without any son at all. He thought of his father, whose greed had put him here. What drove Achmet? Had the tomb itself set a spell on him, drawing him closer and closer until he found that hidden entrance?

Achmet had not been mad before. Had some ancient spirit, lurking in this trap, lured him here and maddened him in order to take his sons? Khalid found he was crying and stopped, for tears wasted water. If he could have willed himself to instant death he would have, but dying of thirst was a terrible way to go.

Strangely, after a time he felt somewhat better. The air did not grow stale. Perhaps some shift in the rock had opened a crack to the outer air. The flame of the single torch he had left alight burned clear and yellow.

Curiosity took hold of Khalid. He would look, he thought, upon the face of the person whose tomb this was. His captor—he wanted to know her. He moved Hamid carefully to a spot against one wall, putting a peacock feather fan over his livid face. Then he pushed the heavy stone lid until it crashed to the floor and broke into three pieces.

The smaller coffin, carved of wood and inset with gold and gems, was easier to open. He laid its lid on the floor, for it was too beautiful to break. He saw the death mask below—pure gold. He lifted it aside and bent over the wrapped mummy, from which a faint aromatic scent still rose, mixed with an even fainter odor of mummified flesh.

Feeling compelled, he unwrapped the yards of rotten bandage, cutting through many layers at once with his knife. When it was removed, he stared down at a withered countenance. Holding his torch closer, he examined the features.

The bones were fine and strong beneath the shrunken flesh. Even teeth grimaced, high cheekbones stretched the leathery skin, and the small chin, pointed and delicate, hinted at long lost beauty.

Khalid bent closer, still under compulsion that pulled him toward that face...and the eyes opened.

There were no eyeballs, but he felt he was observed, assessed... approved? He tried to pull back, to cry out, but he could no longer move. A will greater than his own held him, allowing something to move out of that ancient body and into his own.

Then he cried out in agony, his thin body twisted with pain as it accommodated the terrible essence that had waited for millennia for a suitable habitation. Khalid's mind shrank into the depths of his skull, cowering like a kicked puppy from the thing now wearing his flesh.

A will now inside his body said, "Hush, child! I have waited long, and at last a suitable one has answered my call. You cannot escape. Be still!"

"Why?" his mind pleaded. "Oh, why?"

He felt a grim sensation—a chuckle or a growl. "Vengeance. What else cankers a soul through thousands of years? They killed me and laid me here, with all proper ritual, for they feared me and did not know of the slave who would obey me even after my death. He set the trap, and now they are dust and I still endure, wearing new young flesh."

Khalid could see as the thing rose and moved through the tomb, ignoring his dead brothers and the cobra. As it approached the slab, the stone rose, grinding, into its slot in the roof. The tunnel was dark, but the possessor of Khalid's body moved surely, the eyes of its spirit long grown used to darkness.

A voice from outside cried, "Come out! Oh my son, come out of the shadows!" It held a burden of grief and pain, and Khalid knew the spell had left Achmet, who realized what he had done.

Then Khalid's body emerged into moonlight.

Achmet cried, "Khalid!" and rushed forward. Before he could reach the thing that had been his son he stopped and turned ashen.

The body raised one thin arm. "You are no longer needed," said a voice that was not Khalid's. "Go!" With the gesture, the moonlight rippled like water, and the man sank to his knees and rolled onto his side. The hand he had clamped over his heart flopped limply onto the sand.

"Father!" Khalid had no body, but he still had will. He flung all of that toward the thing holding him fast. A disturbance racked the body that had been his.

"Be still!" came that compelling thought, but he would not. He raged and resisted and rebelled with all his might.

"I will not go with you into our world. I will not see the things you intend to do. Send me out into death, Woman of the Dead! I WILL NOT GO!"

And then he was free, spinning for a moment like a dust-devil poised over the sand, bodiless. Then he blew away across the desert on the moaning wind.

But behind him, forgotten, a thin, twelve-year-old body walked toward the village, ready to deal death and chaos in a new and unready world.

Witches are not all wicked. Some are, indeed, nice little old ladies who love babies.

THE THREE OF THEM

Lacey Temple learned, soon after moving to Drayton, that the park bench under the gingko tree belonged to the three Groome sisters. Nella, Tanith, and Jean sat there on sunny days and obviously longed to sit there on rainy ones, each busy with her own particular handwork.

Nella crocheted fanciful doilies and shawls, caps and foot warmers, making up her own stitches as she went. Few dared refuse the gift of one of her creations, though fewer still made any use of them after accepting. There was something about her bright, steel-gray eyes that daunted criticism and silenced protest. Lacey put her crocheted hat in her closet, under a box of books. Something about it made her head swim, the single time she wore it.

Tanith painted tiny watercolors onto a pad of heavy paper, catching instants of humor or strangeness with her muted tints. She never offered any of her work as gifts, and if someone offered to buy, as happened sometimes when strangers visited Drayton, she smiled and said it would be like selling her child. That was why it seemed strange to Lacey that people feared her more than they did Nella.

Jean, on the other hand, was eminently practical. She mended clothing for the poor, darned socks for her grandchildren, or stitched quilt squares for the annual Christmas bazaar at her church. Of all the old ladies, she seemed the most nearly normal, until you looked into her eyes. There lay madness.

In those black depths, Lacey could fancy a reflection of Fate, wielding the shears that severed body from spirit. When Jean snipped threads or scissored cloth, anyone watching had to flinch.

Nobody gossiped about the three. In a town of two thousand, that was incredible; when Lacey realized it she was stunned. Surely one of the sisters, at some time or another, had to have committed an indiscretion, if nothing worse. Yet the one time she mentioned such a possibility, her neighbor stared at her as if she had lost her wits.

"Not them," Mr. Barrows said in the firmest of tones. "Not them, and you'd better accept that and go on, Miz Temple."

Which, of course, Lacey simply could not do. Having lived in a much larger town before her marriage, she had developed a curiosity about people that only grew stronger when it was denied. The Groome sisters were an itch that was becoming torture.

She studied them for a year without learning anything except the names of their husbands (nobody ever referred to them by their married names, of course) and their children. Their lives were so calm and predictable, Lacey had to accept the universal belief that everything about them and their lives was an open book.

Then she got pregnant. It came as a surprise, actually, for she and Elliott had been married for years without any luck at having children. They had just about given up on it and taken up other hobbies to fill their lives. El golfed on every clear day (and sometimes in the rain) that he didn't have to meet with clients.

Lacey did good works—she helped at the church, volunteered at school benefits, collected donations for the Salvation Army. She didn't much like it, for she had always been shy, but it was better than sitting at home and watching the maid clean the house she would much rather have cleaned for herself. Now she found herself alternately rejoicing and throwing up.

It seemed her neighbors knew of her situation just about as soon as she did. Mr. Barrows and his wife came over with a bouquet of iris. The Curleys, on the other side, contributed an antique baby bed they no longer needed, since Tom Curley had his vasectomy. Everyone seemed to rejoice along with Lacey and Elliott, but the Groome sisters were almost unbecomingly delighted.

Nella came first, bringing a crocheted apron. "Wear this," she said. "It may help the morning sickness."

"Why do they call it MORNING sickness?" Lacey asked her, obediently tying the apron around her still slender middle. "I wake up sick and I'm sick when I go to bed again. I throw up every half hour or so, even when I start the day with dry crackers."

"I've seen such cases before," Nella told her. "You try that apron. Then we'll see."

Strangely enough, the nausea subsided. Not quickly but by degrees it lessened over the next day or two until she could actually hold down a meal. She was actually delighted when Tanith came for her congratulatory visit, bringing a small square package.

Inside was one of the old woman's meticulous watercolors, a baby in a rose garden, laughing amid a drift of cream-yellow petals. Lacey was speechless; never before had Tanith given away a painting, she was certain. Besides which, the baby in the painting was wonderfully realized: it looked like both her and Elliott.

"Miss Tanith, this is lovely!" she said. "Are you sure you want to part with it?"

Tanith nodded. "This is a special time and a special child. We have decided to watch over you and your baby very carefully. Our town is so small...."—she paused as if rethinking what she meant to say—"...so small that few babies are born here. This will be the first in quite a while. Most of us here are retired, for young people move away to the city to get better jobs."

She smiled, and her amber eyes glowed with sudden enthusiasm. "We need young blood here. Take care of yourself." Then she took herself off abruptly, leaving Lacey feeling somewhat odd.

Lacey found herself wondering about Miss Jean. The sisters almost always acted as a team, and where two had gone the third would surely follow. She hung the painting on the nursery wall, framed in cream and rose, and joined Elliott in admiring it almost every evening.

A touch of nausea recurred, but she immediately put on the apron Nella had brought, and it soon went away again. The reason for that was a question Lacey did not consider. There were things about the Groomes that disturbed her placid mind, and thinking about why was something she avoided.

It was well into the second month of her pregnancy when the third sister called. She carried a tissue paper bundle and looked very hot and weary as she came inside. "With the weather so warm, I should have had this sent, I know, but I did want to see your face when you open it," she panted.

Lacey supplied her with a rocking chair and a tall glass of iced tea before turning to the bundle. "What on earth...Miss Jean, you have gone to entirely too much trouble with this, I feel sure!"

"Not a bit of it. I wanted to do something really unusual for your baby. You are Episcopalian, aren't you? You'll have her christened?" Of course she knew the answer, for the Temples attended the small Episcopal church almost every Sunday.

"Yes we will. Did you...oh, Miss Jean, did you make a christening dress for the baby?"

Jean blushed as Lacey cut the strings and unwrapped the tissue, revealing a cloud of white lawn and lace. She held it up, admiring the infinitesimal stitches, the tucks and gathers, the scalloped ruffles, rich with embroidery. "It's a work of art!" she breathed.

Jean nodded. "My very best," she said. "My sisters and I would love, if you have no objection, to be—I hardly know what to call it—perhaps unofficial godmothers? To your baby. Or volunteer grandmothers. We have had no infants to play with in so long, we are most excited about yours."

* * * * * * *

As the time passed (very slowly, Lacey thought), the three old ladies did not lose interest. One or another came at least once a week, bringing herbal teas or bouquets of violets or roses or jasmine, until Lacey felt herself the center of the most adoring attention.

As the ninth month and Christmas approached, she found herself very tired, heavy, and ready for this thing to end. The day before her due date (everyone told her first babies were always late, so she was prepared to be disappointed), all the sisters visited her together.

"We would like to take you out to tea," Nella said. "I know you don't feel up to going far, so we have brought our car. We want you to visit Jean's home, where we have been preparing a special treat for you."

The day was fine, for December. Jean's house, decorated with handmade wreaths and bows and tiny trees in every window, welcomed them in. Lacey found herself relaxing for the first time in weeks. The dread of what was to come seemed to lift, as the old ladies plied her with tiny cookies and fragrant though unfamiliar tea.

"We felt you would do better for an outing," Tanith told her, as she helped her back into their vintage Ford. "Tomorrow is a very special day. Be of good heart, my dear, for we are thinking of you."

How kind they were, Lacey thought as she fell asleep that night. A small town was the place to find true friends...but then she was asleep.

Something woke her in the night, as if a sudden bugle call had signaled action. She rose and began checking her bag to make sure everything was ready; then she went into the bathroom and began scrubbing tile as if her life depended upon getting it spotless. When Elliott woke at last, she knew today would be the day.

"We need to go soon," she told him, as his tousled head appeared around the door frame. "Things are happening."

He disappeared instantly, and she heard him dressing. When she emerged from the bathroom, he had his shirt buttoned crooked and unmatched shoes on his sockless feet. "Not that soon!" she objected.

Before long they were on the way to Heatherburg, where their doctor waited for their arrival at the hospital. With incredible ease, despite what she had read and been told by older women, by eleven o'clock Lacey found herself holding a round-faced girl-child, whose cheeks were ivory smooth, without the usual red blotches of the new-born. A tuft of dark hair crowned her head, and her blue eyes were already wide open, missing nothing. She looked exactly like Miss Tanith's painted baby, Lacey realized.

"What an alert baby!" the nurse said, as she took her up to carry her to the nursery. "She was looking around the delivery room as if she were taking inventory!"

Lacey laughed. A healthy, bright baby was more than she had ever hoped to have.

* * * * * * *

The christening was well attended, and the Groome sisters were seated close to the front of the church. Even there their hands were busy with crochet, paint book, and needle, though they used them very discreetly.

The christening dress looked ravishing, as the priest took small Rose from her father and held her over the font. As the water dripped from his fingers to touch her face, she blinked very quickly. Father Philip flinched as if he had received an electric shock, and Lacey wondered frantically what was happening.

Rose, however, did not cry, and Father Philip finished the service. As the family passed the pew in which Nella, Tanith, and Jean sat, however, the infant turned her small head to look squarely at the three. As they stared back, Lacey felt as if some invisible current flowed between her child and the three old ladies.

Rose gave a chortle of laughter, and the Groomes smiled and nodded knowingly at each other. Lacey was left with the sudden conviction that she had just added a fourth white witch to the coven in Drayton, Texas.

What if a horror writer should be adopted by a ghost?

THE HOUSE ON BOBCAT RIDGE

The accident nearly killed me. Worse, it left my nerves in a terrible state. I'd fall asleep to the sound of city traffic and wake in a cold sweat when my subconscious misread that to be the sound of the freeway off-ramp where a Coca-Cola® truck wiped out my little Saab. I'd wake with my leg aching from pumping a nonexistent brake pedal.

When the need for exercise or groceries drove me out of my apartment, I could hardly force myself to cross a street. Cold sweat would cover me, and I'd start shaking. Usually I'd locate something that would serve my need on the block where I lived and go home again. I got sick of pizza and ice cream, but the grocery is a block away, on the wrong side of the street.

Hank, my long-time friend and doctor, finally took me in hand. When I went in for my check-up, he looked me in the eye. "You look like hell, Loy," he said. "You're not sleeping—I can see it. Not eating right, either. Your eyeballs look like stale meatballs. I asked you to let me know if you had trouble with your nerves, you know. That's not unusual after a bad accident. Quite normal, in fact."

Normal or not, I felt strange about admitting that. He guessed anyway, so I let it all out. I play things close to the vest, ordinarily, but Hank had been my college roommate until I flunked out and went into mowing lawns and trimming hedges, doing my writing on the side.

Hank had always cut his fees to the bone for me, for old times' sake. When I made it big with *Concerto, with Vampires* I made up for it, though. He's been embarrassingly grateful that I dedicated the book to him, as well as catching up back bills he hadn't charged to me.

Now I gave him the truth. "I'm really shot, Hank. No nerve, can't go out into traffic without wetting my pants. The work is at a standstill, too. I'm four books ahead right now, but that won't last with publishers hounding my agent for more work while I'm hot. I'm stuck halfway through my sixth novel, and no ideas are coming."

He nodded and rubbed his chin. "It's nothing physical. The CAT scan showed that your body has recovered amazingly well. Now you need to make your nerves do the same."

I shook my head. "How? I have to live someplace, Hank, and everywhere you go there are automobiles. That's what gets me where I live."

He grinned what I always called his East Texas stump-thumper grin. "I know of one. I go back home every couple of years, just to get the noise and stink out of me. My cousin will rent you his house on Bobcat Ridge, where I can guarantee you'll hear nothing but jet planes and wildlife and crickets."

He chuckled. "If somebody had dropped a bomb on you, I wouldn't suggest this, because those jets streak over and sound like the trump of doom. But that's not a bit like traffic. Outside the desert country or the Northern Rockies, it's the quietest place I know of."

I opened my mouth, but he forestalled my question. "There's a post office five miles away, up an oil-top road that seldom has even two cars on it at a time. There's a grocery store too, but I understand your priorities. Writers live and die by the mail."

"Why doesn't your cousin live in that house, if it's so nice and quiet?" I asked him.

He chuckled. "Old Rich wouldn't be caught dead way down there in the boonies," he said. "There's an old East Texas saying: he's got above his raisin'. Rich would have sold the old farm many times over, if his sister would stand for it, but she says she's going to move down there when she retires from teaching school. Rich fusses, but he can't do anything about it. His Dad knew Rich. The will is iron clad, and Susan has the final say. But the old boy can make a buck renting the place, now and again."

I was at the end of my rope and knew it. I let Hank call his cousin and make the arrangements before I left his office. When I heard the amount of rent, I nearly choked. "What's wrong with it? You can't rent a doghouse for two hundred a month, much less a place with ten rooms, two baths, and a 150 acres around it! Bad water? Sewage problems? Snakes in the closets? I want to know."

"Uncle Ab remodeled the place just before he died," Hank said. "Good well, windmill and tank, electricity. It's just a long way from everywhere. There aren't many people who want to be thirty miles from the nearest movie or club. Now and again Rich rented to fishermen wanting to be handy to the lake, but they really messed the place up."

I'm no outdoorsman. Central Park is as woodsy as I get, but any place with no traffic sounded good to me. I sent Richard Gallery a check for three months rent in advance and packed up jeans and cotton shirts and heavy shoes, along with my laptop, printer, and reams of paper.

Somehow Hank blackmailed his cousin into meeting me at the airport with a rental car. He assured me I'd have to have one, in that isolated area. Actually, I rather took to Rich...he was so obviously a small town establishment crook you could spot him a mile off, and he didn't try to hide it.

In two hours I was driving the car (not even very nervous, because there was no traffic to speak of), following Richard Gallery along a maze of dirt roads. Without a map I might never find the town and the airport again, I felt sure.

We bumped up a track, where two sets of wheels had worn away grass from the gravel driveway that must have been two miles long. The country was, I had to admit, beautiful. In late June the grass was green and tall. Black cows stood in picturesque poses amid all sorts of wildflowers. The air smelled like my grandmother's potpourri, the only hint of exhaust coming from our own vehicles.

Down an incline, through a pine woods we went, and I felt almost intoxicated by the resiny scent. Here I might spend all my time simply breathing. Around a bend, we came out of the trees into a glade stretching up to a low ridge that was crowned with pine and cedar and oak and some kind of bush filled with pink flowers.

The house was sided with plain gray-tan boards, weathered almost to silver. It was big, and a porch curved around the front and left sides, shading a door with an oval panel of etched glass. I didn't blame Rich's sister for wanting to live there.

The door wasn't even locked! Rich looked startled when I asked him why. "Door's never been locked in my whole life," he said. "Out here you don't need to lock things up. There's bolts inside, but the only use they ever got was when Susie and me used to lock each other out of the house, when we were little."

He led me around to the back, where a high curb marked the well. A tall metal frame supported a windmill some fifty feet high, and he showed me how to loose the brake to let it face into the wind and how to pull it down again if the wind rose too high.

"Pump the tank full and drain her a couple of times, to get any algae out. It's been filled a couple of times this year, but it doesn't hurt to have a fresh batch. This valve here lets the water run from the tank to the house."

He opened the back door, lit the pilot on the butane cook stove, and looked around. "That ought to do you. The linens are in the hall closet, and the beds are aired. I get a woman to come in twice a year and see to that." With a wave, he hurried up the hall, out the front, and into his Buick. He left without a backward glance.

Somewhat dubiously I flicked the switch in the room I had chosen for a study. Sure enough, lights came on at my touch. There was a heavy mahogany desk with a swivel chair on clawed feet that grasped green glass balls.

The adjoining room held a bed Queen Victoria would have felt at home in. Its matching dresser had candle sconces and glove drawers—an antique dealer would have drooled over the set. Rich's sister must love it dearly, but I knew why she didn't take it with her. No modern apartment or house could hold the huge and heavy pieces.

I fixed supper, mostly sandwiches and milk, and went outside to sit on the porch. Twilight dimmed the sky, and fireflies glimmered across the meadow, while something called sadly in the distance. I tried to remember the bird imitations Hank had given, to warn me what I might hear.

This one was easy. Whip-poor-will! A squall from the woods made me jump, but it, too, fitted into Hank's repertoire. "Bobcat," I said aloud.

No human sounds interrupted the evening except for a distant "thock! thock!" of someone chopping wood. Only the refrigerator, purring quietly in the kitchen, spoke of the modern world.

I finished my milk, sitting on the cool porch. Hank warned me to work early and late, to avoid the worst heat, for air conditioning was not something Uncle Ab considered important. I went into the study and put my work space into order.

The Creeper from the Crypt had been stalled for weeks. Now, in that quiet, I found the story moving again, aided by occasional yowls or hoots from outside. The story was developing again, and it went like the wind. The grandfather clock in the hall must have had Rich's attention before he left, for it solemnly chimed two as I finished my evening's work.

Feeling a bit foolish, I locked the front and back doors. The windows were screened, and closing them would have made the house unbearably hot, but I made the place as secure as I could. Living in the city makes one very shy about sleeping in an unlocked house.

Warm water soaked the tension from my bones, and I made for that incredible bed. The last thing I saw was the carved gargoyle at the top grinning cheerfully. I grinned back and went out like a light. No traffic noise woke me from a nightmare.

I woke to the sound of a bird going through its entire repertoire, just outside my window. Light was creeping through the vines beyond the screen—I had slept the night through for the first time since the accident. I felt refreshed, invigorated. I just might lease this place from Rich until his sister decided to retire, I thought as I made my breakfast.

I worked in the study until the noon heat brought me to my senses. By then I had a respectable bit of work done, saved on disk and also printed out (I tend to be paranoid). The house wasn't actually that hot—its shaded lawn, high ceilings, and ceiling fans kept it fairly comfortable. When I was on a roll, I felt that I could work all day without too much discomfort.

However, every place I go I absorb for future use. Here I was in the country for the first time, and I was not about to waste the opportunity. I set out for the pine woods with a thermos of water and sandwiches tucked in my laptop bag. Once amid the fragrant trees, my feet cushioned on deep layers of fallen needles, I set my bag on a stump and wandered a bit. A black bird with a raucous voice kept track of my every move, erasing my notion that woods are silent and peaceful. When I stood still I could hear small creatures scuttering among the dead leaves and pine needles, and once I saw a small brown snake flicker from covert to covert.

I went back to the stump and got out the computer. Sitting on the rough-cut wood, I began writing, and a story came out of my head and my hands almost effortlessly. In an hour I had a draft completed, a small gem of some two thousand words. When I straightened my back, I felt someone watching me and turned suddenly.

Something darted behind a tree, but the ghost of a giggle gave me a clue. "Come out and talk to me," I called. "I don't bite little girls. I have a spare sandwich, and I'm ready for lunch."

I gave her time to make up her mind while I rummaged for the thermos and the food. When I turned again, she was halfway between stump and tree. Some trick of the light gave her a strange air, almost translucent in her fairness. Freckled and blue-eyed, she smiled at me and I smiled back, wondering at the old fashioned cut of her gingham dress.

"You want my extra sandwich?" I asked.

Her voice was the merest whisper—"Not hungry...." Her gaze went to the laptop. "See?" she murmured so softly that the hum of bees almost drowned her out.

"I'll set it on the stump. You can read what's on the screen," I told her, backing away.

Looking puzzled, she approached the small screen and stared as if amazed at the words there. "Next time I'll bring the printouts," I told her. "Those are easier to read."

I showed her how to scroll down the pages, and she read intently. When she looked up she seemed more defined, less wispy, and her voice was clear. "Oh, it's lovely! May I have a copy?"

"I'll make one for you tonight and bring it tomorrow. Where do you live?"

She laughed. "You could never find it. I come here every day. If you call 'Lucy,' I will hear you and come."

So it came about that every day I worked and every evening I took printouts of suitable stories or passages from the book to the wood, where Lucy was almost always waiting. We would sit on a log or stump and talk about strange things like going out among the stars or flying with butterflies, and I was amazed at her insatiable curiosity about everything imaginable.

It never occurred to me to wonder how a half-grown child was allowed to wander the woods at will, or how she could have learned about so many things seemingly outside her sphere of knowledge. Often I went all the way to Templeton to the library there, never once thinking about traffic, to find books about subjects that interested her (and me).

At the grocery story one day I asked the owner about my little friend. He frowned. "Nobody down that way has a child that age. Only the Chesters have one at all, and that's a baby. Lucy? Don't rightly know, but you go ask Mrs. Willard. She knows everybody."

* * * * * * *

I knocked on Mrs. Willard's door gently, not wanting to cause the flimsy house to collapse at my feet. Her shuffling step came at last, and she opened the door to reveal lively black eyes in a faded face. Over mint tea in her kitchen, she told me about the people who had lived on Bobcat Ridge.

"Of course. Ab Gallery's folks. I knew the family for sixty years, most of 'em good people except for Ab's uncle Jordan. Meanest man ever lived, he was; quarreled with his kin until his chillen had to sneak off to visit their own cousins. He kept that youngest girl close—wouldn't even let her go to school, but she'd creep through the woods and borrow books from Ab's kids. They said she was brighter than anybody in the school at Brier Hollow."

She sighed, her eyes looking into the past. "She had to hide the books in the woods, else Jordan would've burned 'em. When his wife died, that man went clean over the edge. Locked that poor little thing up in her room so she couldn't get out at all, and she died right there. Just pined away, though she had always been right healthy. Poor little Lucy. She'd be fifty now."

"Lucy...," I breathed. "What did she look like?"

"Oh she was a little thing, slender, with pale hair and big blue eyes. Nicest smile...but here I set bendin' your ear. Tell me what's happening out and away!"

I spent the afternoon catching her up on the wide world, and I got some fine material from our talk as well. But all the while I thought about Lucy, that hungry, frustrated little spirit, still searching the pine wood for books that could not be found.

I had never believed in ghosts, but I believed in Lucy. Unknowingly, I had hobnobbed with a ghost for nearly three months, and now I realized that I had some responsibility toward her. In a week I must leave her to her forlorn wanderings, and the thought was unbearable.

The next day I drove to Templeton again and hunted out a good bookstore, where I picked out books I thought would interest her, as well as classics and things I had loved as a child. I stopped at a hardware store and bought materials for building a watertight cupboard in which to put them.

The next afternoon was damp with misting rain. When Lucy came at last to my call she looked almost as sad as I felt. As she drifted through the trees I saw clearly that she was, indeed, almost transparent, and her blue eyes were troubled.

I swallowed hard. "Lucy, this has been a fantastic summer. I have done more work and better work than ever before. Part of that has been my friendship with you. If I can, I'll come every summer and live in the big house. You will be here, won't you?"

"I'm always here," she whispered. "You have to go? Soon?"

I nodded. "But I have something for you. On our last day together, I'll tell you about my surprise, and the day after I'm gone you go to the big pine tree where I first saw you. My surprise will be there."

She looked up, pain in her eyes, but I smiled. "Trust me, Lucy. I am your friend for as long as we—I—live."

On the last day I put up my cupboard, fixing the door so her wispy fingers could open it. I stacked in the books, writing something on each flyleaf. When I was done, I called her.

Our goodbyes were sad, but she managed to smile and wave as I trudged back up the slope. Once at the house I packed up my things and took one last tour of the house on Bobcat Ridge. It, too, had become my friend. At the door, I spoke to it, foolish as that sounds.

"I'll be back. Wait for me, and, if you can, watch out for Lucy."

She will devour those books, page by page, word by word. I would love to adopt her and take her away with me, but how can you take a ghost from her own place? How can you explain one to a skeptical world? If I could figure a way, I'd do both.

I have arranged with Rich to rent the house every summer. The quality of my work this year is all I need for an excuse. When June rolls around again, I will head back, year after year, if only to rent a room from Susan, when the time comes. I will return to that big house, the scented meadow, and the pine wood.

Lucy will be waiting.

A very long time ago Church officials decreed in Britain that parishioners must be buried in their home churchyards, no matter where they happened to live when they died. This made for real problems for survivors.

THE LYCH ROAD

Rowall woke, as usual, to the pain of his chilblains and the crowing of the scraggly cock in the hen-run. For a long moment, while nerving himself for the icy plunge from his scanty covers into the frozen morning, he forgot what this day would hold.

When he remembered, he went even colder, and as he climbed out of his pallet bed, he shivered with worse things than the early frost. Father was dead.

That was bad enough, in all conscience, but the thought of the effort and the danger involved in getting him to his grave was even worse. Why couldn't the Bishop sit warm in his palace and let poor folk be? What good was served by having men buried only in their home churchyards, when they had lived for sixty years without ever visiting the place of their birth?

Rowall was no coward. Had he not stood fast while hearing the Wish-Hounds coursing over the moors? And had he not even heard, above the whine of the wind and the voices of the spectral hounds, the shrill horn of their master, long dead and held down in his own grave by a great slab of stone?

To travel the Corpse Road was a thing he did not like, but he had done it before, with his Grandsir and his uncle and his mother. And now he must take that way to carry his father too, the long way to his waiting tomb. The Lych Road had no bridges, no post houses, no aids to the traveler. It had only the cold dank miles of moor and the rushing rivers, unbridged and dangerous, and the lurking mists and the mire that lay at a distance, and yet near enough to trap those who went astray in the fogs.

The others had died in summer. That was the difference. Now it was fall, and an early winter was in the nip of the air and the crackle of the frost. If he waited, the ground would be frozen hard, and his father would have to be salted down, as others had been in the past, to wait for spring. That was a thing that edged toward sacrilege in Rowall's mind, and he was determined to get the old man decently underground, if it could be done.

He yelled as he stepped on the flagstone floor. His woolen stockings did little to shut out the chill. Margret thrust her tousled head around the corner from the kitchen, where she slept warm before the hearth, and frowned at him. Then she remembered too, and her eyes grew round as she stared up at her brother.

"Today? It will snow, Gram says. A bad day to be out, at best. And on the moors, it will be terrible cold."

"He must go, else we will have to bide with him in pickle until thaw. The men have given their words to be here by dawn. Go and build up the kitchen fire. They will be wanting something hot in their bellies before we set out. Mull some of the last of the ale...it's little enough we can do to cheer them." Rowall pulled on his awkward hide boots and stood, stamping his feet well down.

The procession set out with first light, under a sky that hung low, in rolls like carded wool. The weather was not, Rowall suspected, going to hold. Not all the way. But at least the rivers might be frozen a bit upstream, holding back some of the flood that had washed away more than one funeral party as it tried to cross the stream.

The wind knifed across the moorland, wailing among the stones, shrieking around the shoulders of Keg Tor, as they drew even with its dwarfish shape. A spit of snow touched Rowall's face from time to time, and the moor itself seemed to dissolve into the gray light of the sky. Even the occasional tree or standing stone was ghostlike in the tenuous light, and the creak of the wagon, toiling away behind, added a shivery note to the day.

Aln, just behind him, touched his shoulder, and he turned. The men pulling the wagon were changing shifts, fresh backs being put to the ordeal of hauling the heavy burden over the stony track. The way ran slightly uphill now, and the box holding his father's body was, he well knew, heavy with its own weight and that of the big bones and loose flesh within it.

He went back and took his place, bending to pull, while others alongside did the same and others pushed from behind. The effort warmed him a bit, though his feet were wet and almost frozen in the ill-made boots. They moved along, the axles groaning, the wind slicing their ears from their skulls and tossing wisps of their long hair about their faces. The day moved too, and it was noon when they reached the worst of the streams.

The Wend had been low enough to cross without trouble. The Pharr was a bit worse, yet passable. Now they neared the Skeg, and they could hear the roar of its waters before they arrived at the high embankment and looked down at the turbulence below. This time, Rowall knew, they must carry the coffin by hand along the water's edge, seeking a way to cross.

The wagon could go at the ford, but it was more likely than not to overturn in the flood. If that happened, the body would be lost, and he had no intention of letting that occur. They would bear it to a crossing, and up the other side, staggering in mud and over icy patches, almost falling back into the stream. He had been there before with the kin of those now helping him. It was a terrible burden for human flesh to accomplish.

It was dark, down in the shadow of the banks. The overcast day did nothing to lighten the shadows, and the footing was perilous. But they persevered, resting the coffin on a stone from time to time in order to catch their breaths and go on. When they found a spot studded with boulders and manhandled the casket across it, they were all weary, and Rowall felt as if he would like to join his parent in the box. His was by far the easiest task.

The farther climb was miles high, it seemed, and the wind, when they reached the top, struck through their rough clothing to freeze the sweat of effort on their hides. But to their dismay, it was blowing snow as well. The way to the road again was covered over, and the moors lay dim and featureless before them.

Aln stood, shoulders hunched, staring toward their goal, still miles away. Rowall knew that he was thinking with dread of the mire below Dredden Tor, which might well lie hidden beneath the light blanket of snow. It had swallowed men and beasts for generations, without returning so much as a rag or a bone of them to their owners and kin.

He sighed. "I will go ahead and sound out the way," he shouted above the moan of the wind. "Keep coming. There is the wagon now, just coming up from the crossing. Load him onto it, and travel onward. I will stop and wait for you if I come to the mire."

In some ways, it was a relief to trudge away by himself into the teeth of the wind, and leave the wagon behind. It had reached a point at which he felt that it was his father himself groaning, instead of the axles and the men. The wind sang a cleaner note into his ears as he forged ahead.

Rowall thought of his grandmother and Margret, worrying in the kitchen as they spun wool and knitted hose and shirts. They might be safe, but he knew they were following him every step of the way. He didn't envy them; at least he knew what was happening when it happened. He thought with longing of his older brother, gone with a drover for a bit of coin to help them through the winter.

He sighed, feeling the chill pull deep into his lungs. It set him to coughing, another of those troublesome fits that had been the bane of his life since fall. He stopped and leaned against a standing stone until he could breathe again. Then he went forward, half blinded by the increasing snowfall.

Something moved in the white blur to his right. He paused and put his hands over his eyes, trying to see. A goat, he thought, or one of the moorland ponies, running from the blast.

He put his head down and went on again, setting one foot carefully ahead of the other, stabbing at the snow with his staff to make sure of the footing. It would not do to stumble into Dredden Mire.

The world went away for a time, as he forced himself onward. He found himself lying flat once, and pushed himself up again, wondering how long he had been lying there. He passed a stone that he thought looked too much like the one he had leaned on hours before. But he was strangely warm now, with effort, he supposed. Nothing troubled his mind, and he walked as if on a summer day, crossing the moors to see his Merry again, forgetting that she had been lost in Dredden Mire months before.

Then he came suddenly to his senses. The ground trembled faintly beneath his boots, as if he stood upon a vast pudding. His breath stopped in his throat, and he clutched the staff in hands that were numb.

He turned cautiously in his tracks. The ominous shape of Dredden Tor loomed to his left and slightly behind him.

"God ha' mercy!" he cried, his voice mingling with the wind.

He turned right around and tried to see his own tracks. He could follow them out of the mire again, he thought, but the snow had covered them over, and behind him was only the regular pattern of windblown drift that lay on every hand.

He thrust the staff at the ground. It sank too easily. He stabbed to right and left, front and back, but there was no difference at all. He stood deep in the mire. Too deep to hope for deliverance. He must have followed one of the meandering strips of solid ground that criss-crossed it aimlessly.

Suddenly Rowall laughed aloud, the wind snatching the sound from his lips. He was relieved of this day's duty, and if death be the price, it was cheap. Merry was gone. His life loomed ahead, labor and cold, cold and labor, until he lay down and died as his father had done.

It was against the law of the Church to die willfully, but accident was another thing entirely. He had been delivered from his fate by his own father's death, it seemed, and he no longer shuddered at his long trek on the Lych Road.

He laughed harder and harder. He plumped down in the powdery snow and lifted his face to the howling sky.

"Bishop!" he shouted, "You cannot say I must return to my own parish for burial! My bones will never be found, Bishop! And my curse upon you for bringing many well men to their deaths in serving those already dead!"

The wind moaned about Dredden Tor, and the mire lay hidden under the snow. The men who hauled his father's lych to its tomb would do their task and some would even grieve for him, he knew. But Rowall did not grieve for himself.

He was growing quite warm, now. And Merry...Merry was coming through the mire in her summer dress, her hands filled with wild daisies....

Our culture discounts children, as people, as witnesses. They know that, and occasionally they impose their own justice.

THE PICNIC

The offshore wind blew hot and dry. Instead of rushing in over the sand beach, the waves sobbed like hiccups against the beach. The Gulf was as smooth as a plate, reflecting sunlight in angry glints as the sun crept westward.

Behind the first array of tall dunes, there was a little dell lined with goats-foot morning glory and sea-oats. A small stand of salt-cedar had found a toehold there, and in its shade a small boy sheltered, burrowing beneath sand and vines. There had been no sound, no call, no footstep for a long while, but he did not dare reveal himself.

Afternoon brought shadows from the higher dunes to the west. The wind shifted to the east, bringing the welcome breath of the ocean. The boy shook off the vines and stood, brushing sand from his almost-bare skin. Despite his efforts to cover himself, he was badly sunburned.

He listened intently, but heard nothing but the lisping waves and the faint hiss of sand against sand. Keeping his head low, he crawled up the dune, his head low, and peered toward the water and the picnic spot on the beach. When he was sure nothing was in sight, he gave a shivering sigh and ran down toward the water.

He could see the place where they had the picnic. There might be scraps, if the gulls hadn't taken them all. His belly was growling, and his knees felt shaky as he approached. He also needed water. He needed his mother...but he would never have her again. She was dead, he knew.

He had been playing in the dunes and returned just in time to see Ralph kill her. His stepfather had given no warning. He seemed no angrier than he ever was after a night of drinking, though he hadn't wanted to go on a picnic.

Pell knew the man was never happy about anything, and he knew his mother was sorry she'd married him, though they didn't talk about it. She kept her troubles to herself. But Pell had seen her die.

He shook his head, dizzy with the blow that had knocked him out, when Ralph realized he had seen. There was a lump on his cheek and jaw that made moving his mouth a misery. He didn't really remember crawling away while Ralph hid his mother's body, but he knew that must have happened.

Moving down the beach, he realized he had reached the site of the picnic. Above the tide-line, he could see a lump of sand covering the thermos. When he shook it, it sloshed.

He'd never drunk coffee, but even bitter as it was, the liquid felt good to his parched mouth. Anything wet was welcome. He dug around the spot near the thermos. There had been a casserole, he knew, and sandwiches in a plastic container. They hadn't eaten them all, he remembered.

When he found the container the food smelled funny and tasted worse. Even peanut-butter didn't keep in such heat, but he choked them down. There was maybe a half-pint of coffee left, but he didn't drink it all. Until someone else came here for a walk on the beach or a picnic, he wouldn't get anything else.

Now the sun was behind the dunes entirely, though it still colored a bank of high clouds. Purple shadow covered the beach and turned the sea deeper blue. Mom had loved to sit and watch the sunset reflected in the clouds.

Pell almost sobbed, but he was ten. Too old to cry. Too old to take what happened to Mom without fighting back. Ralph had hidden Mom's body among the dunes, and Pell had somehow managed to see where. He didn't recall crawling after the man, but he must have.

Ralph hadn't known until he came back that Pell was no longer unconscious but gone. Nobody could find a small boy in the dunes, and Pell knew he'd join his mother if his stepfather found him.

Now he realized he had to go check on Mom. Maybe she wasn't dead. Still, Pell knew better. He'd seen the limp way her neck bent when Ralph lifted her, and her hand swung like the legs of the rabbit Ralph shot last fall. She'd looked dead, but then he probably had, too.

But Pell was alive, and he had to know for sure. If Mom was hurt and couldn't move...he shivered at the thought.

He stopped as a sudden thought hit him. Surely Ralph intended to move her. People roamed the beach and the dunes constantly, and somebody would find her, if he didn't. He wouldn't do that in daylight, but when it got good and dark, the man would come with the car, Pell felt certain.

He knew he had to move Mom again, so Ralph couldn't find her when he looked. He might get rid of her so completely that nobody would believe Pell when he told what he had seen. No, he had to hide her again, so Ralph couldn't locate her easily.

His legs had steadied a bit, and he plowed up the dune and over, toward the spot that was burned into his memory. In a dip between two lesser dunes, Ralph had buried her with sand and pulled morning glory vines over the heap. The vines would have wilted in the heat, so it should be easy to find the place.

The sky was still light, though the sun was down. He found the pile easily and dug into the sand. He touched a shoulder.

"Mom?" He gulped down a sob and made the sand fly. When he uncovered her face it was dark and congested. Dead, without any doubt.

Shaking with grief and fury, he knew he must move her. Ralph was no outdoorsman. He wouldn't stand a chance of finding her. When someone came to the beach tomorrow, Pell could catch a ride and go to the police.

He began scraping away sand, quickly now. As gently as he could he uncovered her and found he was thankful that she was so small. He could catch her under the arms and drag her along. That left a plain trail, but he might have time to brush it away with salt cedar branches before Ralph returned.

He decided to put her as close as possible to the place where they had the picnic. That was the last time they would ever have fun together.... He gritted his teeth and tugged her up the last dune and down the other side to the spot he had chosen. There he dug a small hole and managed to fold her legs up so she'd fit in it.

Pell covered her, smoothing the sand with his hands to make sure it didn't look too much disturbed. Then he went back and swept out the trail.

When it grew dark a half moon was high, and there was plenty of light. The breeze freshened, helping to riffle out the marks in the sand. When he was done, Pell sat beside the thermos to rest. Now he was shaking hard. How had he done this? That was his mother, up there in that shallow hole.

There was nobody left in the world who cared about him. How could he haul Mom around as if she were garbage? Tears filled his eyes, and he cried for a long time, alone on the dark beach.

When he had cried himself out, waves were rushing in with the incoming tide. The moon was bright, and the sea sparkled with diamond points. The breeze was chilly now.

But now Pell knew how he had done what he must. That was their way, his and Mom's. She always said you did what was necessary, and then you sat down and cried or shook or even screamed, if you needed to, but not before things were under control.

The darkness grew thicker, though the beach gleamed in the starlight under the slanting moon. It was time to hide. He wondered how Ralph, with that heart he always complained about, had managed to carry Mom so far and then walk the mile or more to the park where they had left the car.

Maybe he had still been a bit drunk from the night before, but Pell had wondered if that heart business wasn't an excuse not to get a job. Mom's beauty shop did good business, and Ralph never seemed interested in doing anything to add to their income. Pell sat up straight.

What if Ralph really did have a bad heart? He'd had rheumatic fever when he was a boy, he'd told Mom. A new layer of goose bumps prickled Pell's skin as a terrible, wicked, fiendish idea occurred to him. Maybe he WAS a fiend in disguise, as Ralph used to say when he told one of his original horror stories.

He didn't allow himself to plan...exactly. Instead, he climbed around the dune so no tracks would make shadows in the moonlight. He scraped away most of the dirt over his mother. Then he waited.

When he heard the car at last, the only light was that of stars and the white-frilled edges of the incoming waves. Pell peeped over the dune, to see headlights coming in his direction. He'd guessed correctly. Ralph would bring the car as close as possible, so he wouldn't have to carry the body too far.

Pell lay flat as the car pulled to a halt. Now Ralph was backing and turning, positioning the car for his next activity.

"Mom, help me," he murmured as he reached down into the hole and hauled his mother up. She came easily, almost as if she heard him. He brushed away the sand and tried to smooth her hair. There was nothing he could do about her face, but it was too dark to see, anyway. Then he crouched down, hiding behind her.

Pell swallowed hard, trying to loosen his dry lips and his tongue. "Ralph," he called in his boy's treble, much like his mother's voice. "Why have you done this to me?"

The man was in the full light of the headlamps. He looked stiff, turning his head desperately and trying to see where the voice came from.

"Why, Ralph? I was always good to you."

Now the man was looking toward them, and Pell raised his mother's body higher, remaining behind her and keeping his hands under her arms. The stiffness was going out of her now, and her arm moved easily, the hand pointing down toward her husband.

"NO! You're dead—I made sure of it," Ralph choked.

"Of course I am," Pell said, his voice sounding eerie, even to him. "But I want you with me. You said you wanted to be with me always, when we married. Now we will be." Pell moved her arm, beckoning.

There was an odd sound, below. Pell risked a glance beneath his mother's arm. Ralph was down on his knees, trying to pull his shirt apart at the neck. Even as the boy watched, he keeled over onto his side, and his hands clutched blindly at his heart.

Pell laid Mom gently on the sand. Then he went down the dune, sliding to stand beside Ralph. The man was breathing strangely, his throat making odd noises. His eyes were open, but they didn't seem to see him.

Pell pushed him with his foot. "Uhhh," said the man on the sand. His eyes swiveled painfully toward the boy. He gave a jerk when he recognized him.

"Hello, Ralph," Pell said. "Goodbye, Ralph."

He turned toward the car. The man tried to crawl after him but gave up and drew up into a huddle.

As most boys do, Pell had watched people drive. He had no trouble starting the car. Only the long, curving beach stretched ahead, empty of any obstacle. He rolled down the window. "I'll be back, Mom!" he called.

There was a painful sound from the man on the sand. Pell's laugh turned into a sob.

Whatever happened from now on, he knew he could handle it. If he could do what he did tonight, he could do anything at all. He drove erratically up the beach toward the bridge and the town beyond. He knew he would make it.

All the way.

Some of my ancestors came to Texas in the early 1800s. The land and the forest are in my bones and my blood, and I resent fiercely the devastation of the natural systems and the imposition of ugliness here where the Indians lived so long without doing major damage to the land.

THE REWARD

I lay just under the low ridge, my head concealed by a tangle of huckleberry bushes. Even then, I risked only half an eye to watch. In the glade below my position, a dust-devil whirled along the path, growing in strength as it moved, until a huge ant hill interrupted its forward motion. The red grit filled the tall column of the whirlwind; then it moved toward me, as if some purpose guided it. A handful of dust slatted into my eyes, and I ducked to wipe them.

I knew that Noheniche and his people must pass through the glade very soon. I had tracked them, observing their movements closely, and I knew they were on their way to some heathen ritual that took them this way on the first night of every full moon. They were always preoccupied, and I felt they would not suspect an ambush at this particular time.

I had nothing against the old shaman. Still, I was being paid for this task; those who had decided to root out the last of the Naconi and take any lands they had left intended that nobody must be left to dispute their claim. Noheniche was the last and most respected leader of his tribe. Even the President of the Republic of Texas listened to him, and this made my employers uneasy.

When the whirlwind passed, all was quiet below the ridge, but I knew with the sixth sense foresters develop that someone was moving in the wood. I crept a bit higher and peered through the bushes, my rifle sliding forward into position.

This time there were only three. I wondered what had happened to the big scar-faced Naconi who usually came with Noheniche's group. First came the scrawny old woman carrying the usual jar of corn and bag of dried herbs. Behind her was the shaman himself, his tall shape moving silently through the shadows. Even in the fading light I could see his strong, intelligent face as he turned his head this way and that. Did he feel my gaze upon him?

Bent almost double under the weight of a deer came a short, square man I had watched before. He was as quick as a den of foxes and brighter than I liked to contemplate. If I had a problem with this job I expected it might well come from Bobcat-Caller. Still, burdened with the carcass as he was, I decided he might be less of a threat than I had thought.

I thought quickly. With Buck Who Dances absent, my schedule must be rearranged. I must take out Noheniche first, then Bobcat-Caller. The old woman could be finished off last, for she was old and skinny and toothless.

I took careful aim, wanting to kill the old man cleanly. Wounded, he would be more dangerous than either I or my bosses liked. My finger tightened on the trigger, as I centered the sight on that white-haired head.

Something smashed into the back of my head with the force of a mule's kick. My nose broke against the rifle stock. A foot stood on my back, holding me helpless until a pair of hands caught me under the shoulders and flipped me over.

I lay choking on my own blood, looking up at Buck Who Dances. How had he known I would be here? I hadn't gone close to his people in days, for I knew where the shaman's people would go on this night. I had waited here for a night and a day. A shiver shook me, for the black eyes staring down at me were not angry. They were amused.

I tensed, knowing I had to try to free myself, but something struck my head again. The last thing I heard was the slow, deliberate laughter of Buck Who Dances.

Chilly air on my face brought me to at last. I was swaying along, head down, over a shoulder. I could guess whose, and I cursed myself for failing to check out the big man's whereabouts.

I'd been out for a long time. The moon was up, glinting on the back of my captor. I tried to move, but the pain in head and back stopped me, along with a warning pinch from Buck Who Dances. I could feel that my feet were tied, and my hands hung below my head, also tightly bound.

I knew where they were going; I had watched them for three months. Always they went into the big timber near the river, and they always remained there for hours. I'd had no desire to learn more about what they did there, but I felt a cold certainty I was about to.

We passed over the last ridge above the river, and the bottom-lands spread out in the moonlight below us. Now the Indians moved fast, even though it was as dark as the inside of a cougar. In time their steps sounded different, squishing into damp soil, and I knew we neared the water.

They emerged into a circular clearing, where old stumps told me they kept it free of intruding growth. Buck Who Dances dropped me with a thump that made all my sore spots cry out. "So, John Kingman, you are curious about the ways of the Naconi?" he asked in a sarcastic tone.

"For three moons you have watched us, following even to the edge of the holy ground. Tonight, the woman Agoyac tells me, you had your hand on your weapon, ready to kill. Tell the truth, for lies will sting like bees on your tongue."

I may be a hired killer, but I am not a fool. They had caught me, fair and square. I looked up at Noheniche and said, "Ask what you will, Noheniche. I will tell you. Can't do anything else"—and I managed a chuckle. Indians like that sort of nerve.

"Who set you on our track? Why do you deal in deaths that have no meaning for you?" he asked.

This time I really laughed. My nose had stopped bleeding, and my throat was almost clear. In that pool of moonlight, surrounded by miles of unbroken forest, I thought of what brought me here.

"I come from the east, Noheniche. Where the sun rises in the sea, my fathers built their houses, when they came to this country." I wondered for a moment why I was speaking so formally, but then I went on, because the words were there, waiting. "My father was a preacher...you have met his kind."

He grunted, and I detected both agreement and scorn.

"He brought me up to be a preacher too, but I hated that and I hated him, his words and his Book and his whip. I ran away and worked at many things, learning about the forest and its ways. My hands fitted a gun, my eye was true. What I aimed at, I hit. I could trail silently, so I took up death as my trade. It paid a greater reward than life." I was astonished at my own words, for they were entirely true.

"You know who sent me—the men who cut the trees and break the soil and kill the game on what was your land are afraid of the power of your tongue. They want you dead."

"Ahoh!" he said. "You have spoken truly, John Kingman. I see the seed that is your spirit...in other soil it might have borne good fruit. Now it is time for it to be winnowed out.

"Do you wonder how we knew you tracked us? It is simple, for we are greater trackers than you can imagine. How did we know that you waited, though you did not follow us today? That is not so simple.

"Your folk use the land and its gifts, but they do not know them. We are a part of the land; the air and the soil and the water are our kinsmen. They speak to us, and we give to them what we can. Our brother the wind told us you lay behind the ridge. Did you never wonder why he cast sand in your eyes in time to slow your aim?

"Our lives come from the forest and the river, and tonight we brought them the gift of a deer. Yet we find we have a better gift. You will go to feed our kindred tonight."

I looked up, and the moon shone across his face, making it gleam. Any begging would waste breath. Besides, I didn't believe in his earth-gods any more than I did my father's Bible god. If they killed me, it was fair. I'd been ready to do the same to them. If they left me tied, I might be able to work lose before a moccasin or a gator or a cougar got me.

Noheniche looked down, his face sad. "The time of the Naconi grows short. We have lived long and well, and this land has been good to us, but we have no weapons for fighting your kind. We will go away into the spirit-place soon, for the whites will make that happen. So now we ask the land for other things—not game, not good harvests of corn, not many children for the tribe. We ask it for justice.

"We watch your people as they live and work. There is some good in many of them, but that will be overcome by the folly that is also in them. We ask the spirits to punish those who do not love the land. That will not be soon, for the land is patient, yet we believe it will happen in the end. Farewell, John Kingman."

The old woman had been building a tiny fire beside the stream. I could smell the smoke, tanged with nose-tickling scents. As Noheniche stepped away, I could see her sifting handfuls of corn into the blaze. She was muttering some chant, so faintly I couldn't make out the words. The other two men stood behind the fire, quite still, staring at the waters of the eddy swirling in the river's bend.

Noheniche moved toward the water and stopped in the middle of the thin column of smoke. As it wreathed about his body in the moonlight, he looked like a spirit himself. He raised his arms and began to sing, his great, deep voice booming across the river to echo from the trees beyond.

When he paused, he glanced at the other men, who lifted the deer and flung it into the shallows beyond the eddy. Moonlight slithered across the back of an alligator that lay there. It slid into the stream, only its dull marble eyes and the gleam of its ridged back showing in the silver water. The deer disappeared in a boil of splashes.

If another gator that size waited beside the river, and if they tossed me in, that would be the end. I listened to more chanting, as I cursed my limited understanding of their language. The chant ended, and the old woman poured water from a jar to quench the fire in a sizzle of acrid smoke.

Buck Who Dances and Bobcat-Caller came to lift me, carrying me to the water's edge. If there had been a trace of my father's teaching left, I would have prayed, but as it was I went cold and waited for the end.

They set me, tied tightly, against the trunk of a huge willow that leaned its top over the water. They didn't look at me, even as they set me down and arranged me, facing out over the stream. Then they gathered their skimpy possessions and stole out of the clearing, as silent as ghosts.

The moon was overhead, and the water looked hard as metal, the ripples edged with silver. No fish plopped to feed. Not even a whippoorwill mourned in the trees. I stared until my eyes dimmed, but no sign of a gator could I see.

Closing my eyes, I sighed. The willow trunk was rough— perhaps rough enough to scrub through the thongs binding my wrists. I opened my eyes and began to work. And stopped.

In the middle of the polished water, a whirl of mist took shape. Like the dust-devil, it curled upward about an invisible center that could not be wind, for the night was still. As it moved leisurely across the water, the ripples were undisturbed, even when it came ashore. There it paused and grew taller, stronger, more silvery.

My hair was stiff on the back of my neck. Cold sweat trickled beneath my arms. Something inside me was tugged toward the column, sucked like dust toward the force that formed it. My body thrashed, but I was hardly aware. The Spirit called to me, and something in me was answering it.

I was wrenched, torn away from all I knew. The land I had known swirled before my eyes, now bare of forest, even the fields turned barren and dry. The river was filthy, low in its banks.

Nowhere could I see the man-high glades of grass I had ridden through every day. Ugly towns, streaked with hot pavements of stone, seemed to be everywhere, festering like sores amid the remnants of the trees.

I sucked a last breath of air, and it was not clean and pine-scented but tainted with unnatural stenches. That breath left me retching. Then, caught up in the spiraling whirl of the Spirit, I could see below me the cast-off thing that was my body.

At the last, I knew that in the land's good time—or even God's—the prayer of the Naconi would be answered.

What if there occurred a vampire who had incredible self control—
enough to direct his activities, even in his altered state?

I HAVE NEVER
APPROVED OF BREATHING

When you have no physical needs, you find that time stretches endlessly ahead, without even the final stop of death to put an end to it. For that reason, among others, I have decided that writing a journal may serve me well, not only to occupy otherwise empty hours, but also to keep everything clear in my memory.

In this new state of being, there is no measure, so far, of mnemonic accuracy. After all, the brain inside my skull is now technically dead, and I have no indication as to how that will affect such matters as thought processes and long-term memory.

Short-term memory is unfortunately quite clear and specific, although I would much rather forget my sudden translation into this unexpected and unfortunate state of being. As I have been converted into a life-form I had always considered the product of overheated imaginations, the thought of that conversion would give me chills, if I retained that ability. As it is, a purely intellectual tremor shakes me as I think of it...

My brother had warned me repeatedly to avoid walking the city streets at night. As I learned the hard way, New Orleans is no longer a safe place for anyone. Being a country-bred person, used to rambling where I wanted at any time, that stricture bore heavily upon me during my visit with him. The confinement of his apartment was further discomfort; having been lucky in earlier strolls, I decided to risk another.

That was, as you may imagine, a fatal error in judgment. While keeping a sharp lookout for juvenile gangs or drug pushers, I wandered into a quiet park filled with the sweet breath of cape jasmine, where I was efficiently dealt with by what must have been a vampire. Not that I knew it at the time, of course.

The quick swoop of a dark body, the grasp of irresistible hands about my jaw and neck, the sudden stab of fangs took place before I could react, though I am tall and powerfully built. No one human, I maintain, could have done more to resist that preternaturally strong, swift adversary.

Before he had drained my body of blood, I was unconscious, and I knew nothing thereafter for a very long while. Knowing my family, I understand too well the grief my brother and our parents must have felt. I can almost see Arthur, with my mother and father, in the limousine following the hearse that carried my dead body to the cemetery in Metairie.

Too well do I understand the funerals of our clan. Cousins in the slightest degree came, I am sure, to the church for the service, and later to stand with my three immediate relatives at the entrance to the family tomb, their tears mingling with the rain (it almost always rains at funerals, I have found).

Father was, I feel certain, pale as the marble vaults beside the mausoleum. His high forehead was surely wrinkled with grief, although his face would have been composed by an effort of his will. Mother, beside him, would have held her small Bible in gloved hands while she murmured one of her original dithyrambs in classical Greek. I am sure everyone thought she was praying, but I have known my mother too long and too well to believe it.

My brother would have stood, solid as a stump, never betraying his emotions, although it is almost certain that he would have been most upset at this disruption of his teaching schedule. The university might find a family funeral sufficient reason for that, but Arthur Warner would not....

* * * * * * *

I reread what I have written, realizing that I have spent an hour reliving my death and recreating, for my own amusement, the funeral I was not able to attend in spirit, though I was there physically. Although it makes me think I should be sad, thinking about the grief my family suffered, I cannot even manage that much. This new condition is emotionless, as well as being without needs or sensations.

Except, of course, for sudden hunger—but I will save that for later. For now I must put onto paper the accurate progression of events.

* * * * * * *

After what seemed only an instant of blackness, I opened my eyes onto even more darkness. Was my attacker gone so quickly? What had happened to the glimmer of light from the lamp on the corner? And why was it so silent?

I strained all my senses, but even the scent of the cape jasmine was no longer to be found. Instead, there was a musty, fusty smell, a mix of mold and worse things. Had I been taken away, robbed, and dumped into some noxious outhouse?

Finding that my hands could move at last, I felt about myself, trying to find something that would tell me where I might be. Fabric met my right hand as it tried to reach sideways. I felt upward along the surface, which was very cool and dampish, to find that above me was more of the same stuff, its texture smooth but interrupted by regular patterns of quilting or tufting.

Suddenly suspecting what had happened, I kicked outward with both feet, only to have them thump softly against the sides of what I knew had to be a coffin. Had I become so deeply comatose that even doctors believed me dead? And how had I escaped being embalmed? That was the law, and not even the families of objectors could avoid the process. Or did it make any difference?

There was almost no room inside the coffin, no space to gain leverage, but I pushed up with both hands. There was a sharp crack, and the upper part of the lid fell away with a grating noise. I found time to wonder, even in that situation, how I managed it—and then I wondered even more intensely why I was not in a panic, suffering from the classic Premature Burial reaction.

I was not sweating. My heart—and then I began to understand something of my condition—was not beating. I was not breathing. Although the inside of the family tomb was very dark, I could see, as if every old coffin there were rimmed with cold, pale fire.

Terror should have shaken me to my soul, but it was now becoming clear: either I had no soul or it tenanted a lifeless body. I was, lacking any other explanation, a vampire.

There was a certain amusement, chilly and without real mirth, in the thought. I had been an agnostic, skeptic, the coldest of academics! The irony would have infuriated me, but that capacity, too, had left me.

Returning to my coffin by day, after putting the lid back together as well as possible, I found I had no need to destroy it again. I could seep, like mist, through the cracks.

By night, I explored New Orleans, a city of night-dwellers, as few others have done. Until I became hungry...but let us wait for that part. It took quite a long while for that to occur.

I found that getting money was no problem. My strength made it easy to take what I wanted, although a certain remnant of my upbringing limited me to stealing from people I had seen robbing others. There was no lack of those, and some, after suffering my attentions, ran away with such vigor that I wondered if they might mend their ways. It was an interesting thought, if nothing else.

I dropped into the jazz places on Bourbon Street, bought drinks that I spilled onto the floor, and listened with attention, though no remaining appreciation, to the musicians. I wandered through the French Quarter, investigating nooks and crannies my brother had warned me about.

In one street down by the wharf, I found three young men beating another, obviously with the intention of killing him. Drifting up behind the enthusiastic trio in the manner I found had become natural to me, I lifted two by their necks and flung them against the adjacent wall. The other glanced up, caught my eye in the dim light, and sped away without worrying about his companions.

Their victim looked up at me, his eyes wide and appalled, and fainted. I wondered how I looked when angry, but being unable to find any reflection, whether in store window or in looking glass, I could not say. I envisioned Dracula, though without a cape. Not a bad image, I thought.

The police wondered why crime diminished in the French Quarter over the next few days. I found I liked the sensation of being a sort of Superman, protector of the underdog, and I hunted the streets every night, reading about my nightly escapades in the next day's newspapers.

CRIME RATE DROPS, said the *Times-Picayune*. "Murder rates have decreased in the French Quarter by two-thirds, and robberies by half. Police are puzzled, although city officials claim this is due to regulations imposed by the new administration."

I laughed. Living or dead, politicians could find my funny-bone. And that was when I felt the first devastating surge of hunger.

* * * * * * *

I was a boy once. I read all the standard horror fare, including *Dracula*. I knew what that hunger meant, and it was repugnant to think of doing to others what had been done to me. No, I must find a way both to satisfy my hunger and my conscience (which I found interesting, for the literature implied that conscience would be gone past remembering).

Still suffering terrible pangs, I retreated to my coffin in the cemetery in Metairie and ruminated there for a very long while. Control is the hallmark of the Warners, and even in this strange condition I found I had retained that ability, holding myself down by total concentration of will,

I did a lot of serious thinking over the next two days.

On the third night I rose from the coffin and wafted through the cracks into the balmy night, my decision made. It was possible, I found, to move swiftly, in the misty form I could assume, going wherever I wanted. That suited my purposes very well.

I went, on that first night, to the home of the man I had heard named, on one of those nights of wandering, as a kingpin of the drug trade. I went to the door just after dark and used the griffin-headed knocker to summon a neat black maid.

"Could Mr. LeBoeuf spare a moment?" I asked.

Dressed in my best black suit, which for all my activity was un-soiled and unwrinkled, I knew I looked respectable. When I was not indulging my penchant for violence, I must also look normal, I had decided long before, for waitresses and bartenders had not looked at me twice.

She looked doubtful. "I'll ask him," she said. "Your name?"

"Evans Warner," I said without thinking. But LeBoeuf would not know the name of an obscure professor of literature, I assured myself. "I have a small...proposal...for him."

She smiled and closed the door. In a few moments she returned and beckoned me into a big room filled with computer equipment and Nintendo games. The drug lord sat at a desk, his face awash with reflected color from the computer screen before him.

He looked up, frowned, and said, "If this is a joke, be sure it makes me laugh. I never thought I'd get a visit from a dead professor, but now I have. What's the scam?"

I smiled as I closed the door behind me and turned the old fashioned lock. "No scam," I said, even as he reached for an alarm button.

He hadn't a chance, for I was faster and far stronger than he. I had him by the neck before he could do more than gasp, but it was not my purpose to create more creatures like me. I broke his neck and then, while the blood was still hot in his veins, I drank my fill.

* * * * * * *

Although, when I am active, life holds a certain interest, the hunger does not occur frequently. That is why I sit here in the dimness of the family tomb, or sometimes on a marble bench in the moonlight, and write in this journal. Between hungers, I find this life incredibly boring.

However, as a result of my selective feeding, New Orleans is now becoming one of the most crime-free cities in the U.S. The newspapers, which I continue to buy and read from beginning to end, marvel at the rash of deaths that has removed most of the major criminals from their various despicable trades.

They are properly sarcastic concerning the name of the man who killed François LeBoeuf, of course. A thoroughly respectable academic, dead these three months, cannot be held accountable for the actions of some madman who gave his name to the maid. The fact that all the dead people, women as well as men, were found to be dangerously anemic is not mentioned in print.

I find that amusement is the only sensation left to me, aside from the occasional dreadful hunger. If I must be a creature of the night, doomed to live forever and to kill others along the way, it seems that I have found a useful and productive way in which to do it.

It would be very pleasant, I think, to visit my old haunts—oh, a dreadful pun!—and see my kinfolk again. However, that is a thing I do not quite dare to do. They would know my face, certainly, and it would trouble their hearts more than I care to see.

And who knows? I might become hungry. My control might slip. I do not want or desire company on the lonely and endless road I must travel. And not even my mother, strange as she sometimes seems, would welcome a life such as mine.

Here is another what if—what if a victim suddenly finds herself awake and driven to exact revenge?

THE AWAKENING

Alice had never thought to travel this road again, moving on numb feet along the frozen track, while thin veils of blown snow buffeted her body and obscured the footing. Only hatred compelled her, its dwindling yet still urgent flame giving her the strength to climb the path beside the signpost and begin the long struggle uphill.

She trudged along doggedly, slipping on the frozen patches of gravel and sometimes pushed backward by a particularly vicious gust. Her memory had been damaged by the thing done to her body, yet it retained enough purpose to push her onward. Something called her irresistibly toward the one who had stolen her life and her soul.

The light was almost gone, for heavy cloud veiled the sinking sun. If she had been as she was before, she might have sunk into a frozen lump and died there on the path, but that ability was lost in the past. Now she only moved, a small pillar of hatred, toward her goal, which was drawing nearer as she topped the rise and started down into the weedy grounds sloping away toward the river beyond the ruined manor house.

Through the blowing snow, Alice could see gray snaggles of stone towers that rose above the house. Peering through the twilight, she could see no hint of life or light, but she continued downward, her feet slipping on the icy gravels of what had been formal paths, on this side of the hill.

Stiff trees, unpruned for decades, overhung the path now, and bristly scrub intruded upon its width. The quarrelling of rooks came dimly to her ears as she approached the grim doorway of the servants' hall, whose lintel had tumbled backward into the hallway beyond.

How long had it been since she stood here, a timid child of a serving maid led by the stern housekeeper into this new place of employment? There were great gaps in her memory, though she recalled the faces of her kin. She had wept when she left her mother and the small ones, but the promised wages meant survival for her family. She had not thought to find death waiting there.

She paused, stunned by a rush of memories. The young master...yes. He had come to her bed, but not to tumble her as she had been warned. Her last clear memory was of his cold lips against her throat.

Then there was darkness, from which she had awakened only a short time ago. How long? Days and nights no longer had meaning for her. Long enough for her to walk from her home village, which had been two days' distant by coach from the manor of the Carville-Antrims. She could not remember how long she walked, but she did know there had been no need to sleep, eat, or rest.

She rubbed her hands together, wondering how to enter where she must go. The crypt was below the chapel, in the depths of the ruined pile before her. How could she get there? Although she had no logical reason, she knew she must find the one who summoned her, though he had been her tormentor, if she was to find ease or rest.

Mold rolled up between her fingers, and she stared down, puzzled. How had she become so dirty?

Digging...the word floated to the surface of her damaged mind. Digging upward, after breaking out of the rotted wood of her coffin, to push her way into the damp air of the churchyard in a weird reversal of birth.

She sighed, and for the first time really understood that she had not been breathing. All the frightening tales told by the grannies in her childhood rushed into her mind, and she cringed against the cold wood of the door. Why had she been called to this place? What further service did that terrible man demand of her?

Something creaked, and the heavy door dropped into the darkness behind it. Her way opened into a musty, cobweb-infested tunnel that wound amid fallen walls, dropped ceilings, and moldy remnants of furniture.

As she scrambled like a mouse through the ruins of the house, Alice wondered at herself. The grannies said those who were like her could not bear the light of day, but she had walked through day and night for a long time. They said that the undead could not die, except in prescribed ways at the hands of the living.

There were tales claiming that those who were caught and sealed with signs and spells could never come forth again, except if someone freed them from their prisoning tombs. Could that be the purpose that had waked her from her sleep? Nevertheless, something within her told Alice that she could free herself, if she held firm against the compulsion that had seized her body.

Avery Carville-Antrim—that was the name, that was the face, that was the will that kept her on her way. What she might do when she found him was unclear, but Alice felt she would know when the time came. As mice scuttered away from her intrusion, as rats bared sharp teeth and spiders draped themselves and their webs about her rotted clothing and struggling body, she held his image clearly before her inner eye.

There had been warnings in the kitchen and the scullery. Other wenches whispered about the son of the house, his unorthodox dalliances with the prettiest, whether willing or not, and the disappearances of more than one of those girls below stairs who had received his attentions.

Alice had been the youngest of them all, fourteen when she came to Carville Manor. She had been pretty, she recalled vaguely. Or others had said so. For two years she had lived and worked in the scullery and the servants' quarters, never coming into contact with the Family. When she was sixteen she had been promoted to chambermaid, and that was when Avery saw her.

She reached an interior place where the rubble was held back by stone walls and the stout upthrust of the main chimney stack. The Hall—she could still see, with her altered vision, vestiges of tapestries against the walls, tumbles of rust that had been armor in the corners. The great maws of the fireplaces at either end yawned black, even in the consuming darkness.

The chapel was at the end of the corridor beyond the Hall. It, too, should be intact, for it was small, its walls thick stone, its roof groined. The altar was high, a solid monolith, she remembered, with the thick book she had assumed was a Bible lying open atop it.

Now she wondered what the book had actually been. Not a Bible, she was certain, though she could not recall what the priest had said, when the staff was herded to services by the housekeeper. His words had been alien to her ears, and no one had ever translated them.

The corridor was thick with dusty webs, but she pushed through them without revulsion. No spider could alarm her now, though she had feared them in her other life. She did not sneeze—those who do not breathe do not mind a bit of dust.

The arched doorway into the chapel was open, the doors collapsed into splintered halves, as if some violent force had wrenched them apart and flung them down. To her changed eyes, the vaulted room seemed filled with crepuscular light that seemed to emanate from its center. There the stair to the crypt lay beneath a heavy stone inscribed with Latin words she had never understood.

She moved silently over the dust of years to stand beside that door. The iron ring that was its handle was no colder than her hand when she gripped it and lifted the thing as easily as if it had been made of light wood. She was stronger, now, than she had been in life. That was a valuable thing to know.

The calling intensified, a longing to be free filled the chamber as she approached the door. He waited there, knowing she came to free him from his tomb, but something inside her disputed that. She looked about for some weapon, for what she would find in that tomb would be far stronger than she.

There was an ancient chest pushed against a wall behind the altar, and she lifted its lid and looked inside. There lay the fitments of the chapel, left from the time when it had been used for its original purpose. Candlesticks, incense pots, a great cross of silver, tarnished black, moldy vestments left by long departed priests.

The cross—she should not, according to the stories, be able to touch it without agony, but it came into her hand, its weight promising to make it a usable weapon. Each arm of the cross was pointed, sharp—her instinct told her that would serve her purpose, and she carried the thing back to the stair and began descending into the crypt.

The weight of her weapon was no burden to her lifeless muscles, and she went down swiftly now, so near her summoner. She felt a presence there, knew that he lay there trapped, perhaps by some powerful compulsion set by a person he had used or terrified.

Her vision had adapted to the lack of light, almost seeming to provide its own illumination. She reached the bottom of the shallow steps, and looked about at the tombs that stretched away into darkness on all sides.

Ornate, decorated with laurel wreaths, flowers, crosses, draperies of stone, they held the names of ten generations of Carvilles and Antrims. The Master she had come here to serve must also lie here, with his long-dead wife and the son who had become a monster.

"Avery," she murmured, her voice seeming to stir the veils of webbing like ripples of breeze. "Where do you lie, Avery?"

Though she could not read, she searched among the tombs, looking for the one that had called to her across the terrible miles, bringing her out of her grave when the time was right. Still she wondered why she had come, why the old tales of helplessness, once claimed by the undead, did not seem to control her completely.

What was the compulsion that had brought her to this place of death? She did not know, but could only follow the call that had carried her so far. She found now that the flame of fury burning within her seemed to intensify.

Winding among the standing tombs, she moved farther into the darkness, feeling some invisible connection drawing her toward the one she sought. Small creatures scattered before her, mice chittered in crevices, insects scrabbled and skritched as she went, but she did not slow until she stopped beside the last tomb in the newer part of the crypt.

Also of stone, this held no ornament, no carven cross, no Latin words. Only one name. A-V-E-R-Y, she spelled out with difficulty. The name was surrounded by an intricate pattern like a chain, but composed of runes like those on the standing stones near her home village; they circled to meet the same design wrapping the sides of the stone box.

Here he lay, that monster of the night. She had reached her goal. Now her task must become clear, or she must lie here and wear away eternity among those who had abused her.

She felt something within the tomb become alert, aware. The summons became painful, and she knew she must open the stone, free the monster within it into the world again. Yet that other self, the angry and despairing child she had been, did not release its grip upon her.

Alice wedged a point of one arm of the cross into the seam between the lid and the main tomb and pried. The slab of stone slipped aside, and she pushed it hard, sending it crashing onto the flagstone floor, where it broke into halves, shattering the chain-pattern beyond retrieving.

Climbing onto the plinth that held the tomb, she peered down into the gloom of its interior. The glint of eyes stared up at her, and the pallid face of Avery Carville-Antrim stared up at her with dawning glee. The lips stretched into a grin, showing those sharp white teeth that had ended her life. Even as she looked, he began to move, to raise his skinny arms and lever his torso upward.

That lid she had removed, with its chain of runes, had been the only thing holding him here where he belonged. Now he would go free again into the world. Something deep inside her could not allow that to happen.

Alice heaved the heavy cross high above the tomb, and Avery laughed, a thick chuckle that mocked all the things lesser beings believed about the efficacy of the symbol. But she did not try to control him with it—no, Alice brought the thing around in a powerful swing, and the point of one arm struck into the heart of the monster in the tomb.

No fountain of blood gushed—it had been too long since the thing had fed. A guttural croak, a gurgle of agony, and a whisper of limbs stiffening and straightening against rotted grave clothes were the only sounds in the crypt. Then the shape in moldy cerements began to shrink, until it was less than dust.

As it dwindled, Alice felt herself grow faint. The light dimmed, as her eyes lost their preternatural sharpness. Her tattered flesh thinned on her bones, and she fell from the plinth to lie in the age-old dust.

She knew now what she had truly come to do. In destroying the monster, she had freed herself. Now she was no longer trapped in dead flesh; her spirit could seek for whatever came beyond the term of life.

The dust settled about her, spiders moved on their many-legged ways across her still body, but the spirit that was Alice was no longer a prisoner or a victim. That went free into the clean realms beyond the physical world, while a moan of outrage and despair rose above the tomb marked with the name of Avery Carville-Antrim.

A lifelong claustrophobe, I find the idea of being trapped below-ground the ultimate horror. This is a mean *story!*

DOWN IN THE DARK

He sat on a cold damp stone and listened to the drip.

It seemed impossible that a single drop of water falling onto the stone could set up so many echoes, distortions, and hints of distant voices as this one managed to do. It was all too much like the Chinese water torture.

He shifted uneasily on his chilly perch. To reassure himself, he reached out to touch the solid stone against which he leaned. Being in such total darkness messed up his sense of direction and even his balance, and he needed to make contact with something solid and relatively vertical from time to time.

For that reason, he found himself moving about less and less. It had been hours (or days?—surely not weeks!) since he had been trapped in the cave. But along with the lost headlamp, the rope, and his sole companion, he had lost his sense of time.

He thumped his fist against the stone and cursed softly. He knew better than to go spelunking alone. So did Charlie. They'd been taught always to have someone topside who knew where you were and could bring help if you went overtime. They knew not to go into unknown tunnels without a backup system. They had known that!

But he and Charlie had been so cocksure, so bone-headed. And now Charlie was lying against the rocky spur someplace off to the left, with his head bashed in after they both had fallen down an unsuspected shaft. If these depths hadn't been so constantly cold, he would be stinking right now,

Harrison knew.

Even that would have been something for his deprived senses to work on, Harrison realized with horror. Except for the feel of the stone and the dead-still, dank air, the anonymous scent of rock, and his own aftershave there was nothing. Not really. That inexorable but faintly nasty smell was probably his imagination.

He ran his tongue across his teeth, but the taste of his own mouth was too familiar to help him any.

Charlie had carried the pack with the lunch and the water bottle. Someplace in his plummet downward, he had lost his hold of those. Harrison, falling safely into a patch of sand, had searched his friend's body frantically, once he knew there was no way out, but not even a broken strap remained fastened to the limp shape that had been his closest friend for nineteen years.

Harrison squinched himself into a knot on the rock. He'd avoided moving around since he found this spot where he could be relatively comfortable. The niche had become familiar, over a period of time, and if he should lose track of it—he shivered at the thought. That made him reach again to feel the rough stone beside him. Then he leaned his head onto his arms and drifted off to sleep.

A sharp sound woke him, he thought, though it was so mingled with the remnant of a dream that he couldn't be certain if it came from inside the cavern or from inside his head. He strained his ears, hearing only the drip. Then from someplace near at hand there came a rushing sound. Not water...it wasn't that sort of sound. There was thumping mixed in with it.

He quivered with concentration as he listened. Then he gave a short bark of laughter and stood up. It was his own blood, rushing through arteries and veins. And the thudding was his own heart. Those familiar things had sent him into near hysteria. He leaned back carefully against the rock and began to sing loudly. Anything was better than hearing that drip, though he was no singer.

Without thinking about it, he began a song his Polish grandmother had sung to him as a child:

> Down in the dark where the Kobolds play,
> Down in the dark where it's never day,
> Down in the caves where men dig for ore
> Miners go and return no more.

He caught himself, realizing what it was that he was singing. That was no song for a man trapped underground! He shuddered as echoes bounded away along invisible and unguessable corridors. Then they came back it him from strange angles and impossible directions.

"Harrison Gramme," he said aloud, ignoring the mocking voices parroting his words, "You've got to pull yourself together.

Mom will realize that something's wrong. It can't have been days or weeks. I'd be starving by now. She'll send help—figure it out—you'll see!"

Heartened by his own words, Harrison straightened his back and tried to get some sort of bearing on his present position. "Charlie's off to my left," he said. "The pack of food and water should be someplace around the spot where he landed, even if I couldn't find it before. I must go very cautiously over this entire area. It has to be here. If I do it right, I should find it."

He didn't trust the footing. The floor of the cavern was a tumble of fallen rock. He went to his knees and began crawling to the area where he thought Charlie lay. The chunks of rock bruised his hands and his knees, but he persisted. When his hand touched something cold and rubbery, he stopped, his heart thudding.

Then he knew—it was Charlie's hand. It wasn't stiff—did that mean he hadn't been dead long enough for rigor mortis to set in? Or had it been so long it had already left his body? Harrison found himself thinking of the many arguments he'd had with his mother over his love of mystery stories.

Now he said aloud, "You see, Mom? You said nobody ever learned anything useful from a murder mystery. And here I've found this is very useful, even if I don't quite know what it means. I told you I wasn't wasting my time."

As the echoes answered, he began moving, keeping Charlie's cold form on his left. He crawled in a circle, reaching from time to time to touch Charlie, making certain he stayed within the spiral pattern he'd decided upon. One circuit. No pack. Another circle, wider, this time. Still no pack.

He went around and around, finding it easier to move in a curve than it had been to try traveling in a straight line. Now and again he moved back far enough to locate Charlie, so he couldn't inadvertently move away down some invisible tunnel. On the fifth time around, or the eighth or the umpteenth, he couldn't tell for sure, he set his hand on something dampish. Soft. Neither stone nor dirt. It was the pack.

He fastened it to his belt with the remnant of the strap and crawled back toward where he hoped Charlie lay. After casting around for long minutes of anxiety, he found that limp hand again. He oriented himself by Charlie's body and that allowed him to take off for his rock and his corner.

Once there, he laid out the pack, finding the water bottle intact. He was even thirstier than he had thought and had to control his urge to gulp the entire content. Obeying instructions far too late, he sipped slowly and recapped the bottle.

The sandwiches were squashed and soggy, but he ate one with good appetite. His stomach seemed queasy at accepting the food, but the taste gave him something to think about besides the drip. He savored the aftertaste for a long time. Then he was back to the darkness and the drip.

While he'd been busy with the pack, he had been in pretty good shape. Not the greatest, granted, but he hadn't had time to think. Now, in the back of his mind, the song began going round and round: "Down in the dark where the Kobolds play...."—until he shut it off with a physical effort.

There was nothing more to do. In this deeper layer of the caverns, it was worse than useless to crawl around looking for a way out. Even at the point when he and Charlie began their disastrous slide downward, they had been hundreds of feet from the surface.

So he sat. The drip plipped and plopped until he could see bright circles of color go rippling off behind his eyes at every drop.

After a while he slept again. This time he slipped off his rock and lay curled on the rough floor. Technicolor dreams pursued each other through his sleep. He woke while explaining to his mother why he was so late in returning home.

They hadn't brought much food to begin with. He found that it wouldn't stretch to more than three meals, even tiny ones that weren't more than snacks. When the last morsel was gone, he cried... not because he was hungry. He hadn't really been hungry since the fall. He knew he would miss the act of getting out the food and chewing it. And the taste!

The water lasted longer. When it was gone, he sat on the rock in despair. He'd never find the source of that drip—it was probably high up anyway. Nobody would come. Nobody could come, for he and Charlie hadn't told anyone exactly where they were going. Someone would have tried to stop them, for this complex of caverns was dangerous, and had not been thoroughly explored. Now he wished devoutly that someone had stopped them.

He knew he was sitting in his grave. He had known it all along. Tears slid down his cheeks, and he put out his tongue and tasted the salt.

Time slipped past, dragged past, ground past with agonizing slowness. Once he crawled over to make sure that Charlie was truly dead, not just unconscious. The marble texture of his flesh was enough to convince him.

Then Harrison slipped into a sort of daze.

When he came to, he was certain that men with torches were coming up a long tunnel. He was on his feet, calling out to them. The bright vision vanished. He sat again, dozed, and found himself talking to Charlie, just as he had always done. His own voice woke him, that time. It frightened him badly.

"I've got to hold onto reality," he said to himself. Now the echoes were becoming friendly and comforting.

Once more he sat, straining his ears. The drip had become so familiar that it was now inaudible. He began to hear—or to imagine he heard—faint movements in the deeps about him. A tocking noise, like a hammer on stone, reached him. Something grated across the rocky floor.

Harrison pinched himself, touched the rock, reached down to feel the texture of the pack. He felt that this time it was no illusion conjured up by is deprived senses. He thought he could hear activity going on in the depths of the cavern. Who? What? He laid his head again onto his arms.

"Down in the dark...." He shook himself savagely. Kobolds, indeed! Old country superstition. Then he thought of all the things that might really live out their lives in the deep places of the world. He knew there were eyeless fish in underground rivers—he'd seen some on a class expedition. He knew from experience that things were always scuttling, jut outside your circle of light, when you explored dark deeps.

Bats, of course, but this was too deep for them, he thought. What animals could possibly live here? Or...Kobolds...?

His grandmother's people were miners in the old country. She had told him tales of phantom hammers deep in the mines. Strange things appeared to miners, she said, including her own grandfather. Strong, capable men disappeared and were never seen again. Her song had been a miner's song.

His mother had objected to the old stories. Now they had returned to haunt him.

He huddled on the rock, hands limp in his lap. His eyes were wide, straining to see into the blackness. Time and space didn't exist for him any longer. He was surrounded by invisible somethings that his imagination tried to provide with shapes. What could possibly scrabble and hiss around him? Or was everything inside his mind, scratching and burrowing in his brain?

He heard footsteps, crunching in the pebbles of the floor. Something was coming, he knew! Something he couldn't face—he whimpered, covering his head with his arms, burrowing his face into his lap. Darkness swirled up in his mind, smothering him with terror.

Deep inside him, he heard the words, "Down in the dark where the Kobolds play...."

And he never, ever heard the voices calling to him from far above his head.

I have known too many veterans of the Vietnam War who returned with great damage to body and soul. Back in the Eighties there was a series of unexplained deaths among Vietnamese refugees. This is my explanation of one of those.

CAGE OF THE HEART

I shrank in upon myself, huddled in a corner of the bamboo cage. The rods that formed it were a black web against the dim light from the low doorway of the hut; they offered no concealment to any prisoner kept there.

I could hear Dien's boot heels tapping down the walkway between the huts as he came after me. Again. He always came at twilight.

I throbbed with remembered as well as anticipated pain. I felt as if I were some injured organ cowering inside the ribcage of a tortured creature, helpless to prevent its coming agony and anxious to plead with the host-body, "Tell them what they want to know! Give them anything they want! Just get us out of this!"

I knew that was useless. Dien wanted nothing that I could give him, for I was only a lowly infantryman. I didn't know anything of value to his superiors, and he knew it. Dien enjoyed giving pain.

I shivered harder and harder. If I had possessed some honorable reason for my suffering, some heroic stance that justified enduring the torture, it might have helped, just a bit. And then again, it might not.

I was shivering so hard that the rattle of my cage was drowning out the tap of the approaching boots. My hands clenched, and my jaws locked together until my teeth ached.

* * * * * * *

I woke with a jerk, as always, and stared blankly at the pattern of light and shadow on the bedroom ceiling. I was still shaking, and Dorothy was beginning to sigh, preparatory to waking.

Sliding from the bed, I padded toward the bathroom. On nights like this, when the shaking started, I tried to leave our bedroom before I woke her. It frightened her almost as much as it did me, and that bothered me almost as badly as the recurring dream. I slept many a night on the couch in my study, after a dreaming encounter with Dien.

I stood over the toilet, refusing to look down. Dien had done things to my plumbing that still had not healed and probably never would. There was often blood in my urine. I stole a glance and saw that it was back again. Oh, great! Fumbling in the medicine cabinet, I got out my medication and took two. My hand was shaking, and I gripped the edge of the basin to steady myself. What a wreck that devil had made of me!

My hands, revealed in the harsh light of the bathroom fixture, were sickening. Scarred, crooked-fingered, their nails still misshapen from the insertion of bamboo splinters, they had been hard to force to learn to type again. It had required long and painful effort, and the sight of those gnarled claws still made me sick and angry.

I had been no model soldier, showing great endurance and fortitude. I remembered that with shame. I had wept and shrieked, along with the rest of my hapless fellows who had the misfortune to fall into the hands of Dien. Most of the others had died. I had missed that death by minutes, for the chopper had come as I was being marched out to the killing place.

I gulped air and stood erect. If I'd been a coward, so had every other man in the compound. Nobody could out-tough Dien, and nobody had tried to for very long. And now I was free. At home. My articles were selling even better than they had before I went to 'Nam, and I was writing better than ever before.

I'd be damned before I would go to a shrink for help. That would be the final and shameful cowardice. A copout that I wouldn't let myself consider. I had always solved my own problems, except for the problem of Dien, and there had been no possibility of dealing with him. When you are starved and beaten and bleeding, it's all you can do to hold yourself together enough to keep going.

Once I lay down on the couch, I stopped shaking. Usually I slept pretty soundly after one of those dreams. I seemed to have only one really terrible Dien dream per night allotted to me. Once I finished with it, I could sleep, though I didn't go back to bed for fear of waking Dorothy.

* * * * * * *

My next article was scheduled to cover one of those little towns north of Houston. I was doing a series of pieces on good places to live, if you worked in the city but didn't want to live there. Cane Creek had a neat downtown area, whose storefronts had been modernized. There was a good selection of shops. The merchants were cheerful and friendly.

I forgot the night before, for I loved my work and put everything I had into it. My articles were popular, I think, because I never skimped research or painstaking effort in preparing them.

I'd just come out of the bank and was moving toward the drugstore when I saw Dien. He was walking along, totally assured, leading a small dog that looked like some rare and expensive breed to me. A short dark woman was beside him, and I also recognized her. Her photograph had been on his desk, each time I had been dragged into his office at twilight. The Chamber of Horrors had adjoined his office, and her face, as well as his, was etched into my memory.

I stopped in my tracks, so quickly that an elderly woman almost walked into me. I smiled absently as I apologized, but all my real attention was focused on the pair as they entered the bank I had just left.

Once I was in the drugstore, I asked the druggist about the two Vietnamese I had just seen. "I was in 'Nam, and I could recognize a Viet anyplace," I explained.

"Ah. Yes. The Nguyens. A hard-working couple, those two. We wondered a bit, when they first came, if they would fit in, if it was going to work, having them here, but they have really made a place for themselves in Cane Creek. Mr. Drake, they are the thriftiest people you ever saw. In five years, they have paid for a big farm and found markets for their produce. Why, they're well-to-do now. We're really proud of them."

"So they live here? Interesting. I may put something into my article about this being a very open-minded community, as well as its other virtues," I said. "Where do they live, do you know?"

"Oh, yes. Their farm is about five miles out of town on the farm-to-market road running northeast from the bypass. They have hired a bunch of their relatives that made it over to this country, and those people grow more vegetables on that acreage than you would believe. The others never come to town, so I don't know them personally, but I expect they are as good as the Nguyens."

I felt a chill along my backbone. I had seen how Dien enslaved the local Vietnamese when he ran the prisoner camp. Unless he had changed a whole hell of a lot, he was working a lot of boat people as slaves. I would have bet anything on that.

I took my leave of Mr. Simpson rather hurriedly. I wanted to get out there to that farm while the Diens were in town. They hadn't come out, so I knew they were still in the bank.

I found the farm without too much trouble. A stand of pines almost hid the house from the road, and I drove past the neat driveway to a track that led into a field through a thick stand of bushes. I parked, leaving the car hidden, and scouted back through the pines until I could see the house and a good bit of the cleared land behind it.

The soil had been turned for a second planting, though it seemed late to me to be planting anything. Summer just about burns crops to cinders in this latitude. Small shapes bent above the rows. They weren't wearing coolie-hats, but they had that stoop-backed posture I had come to know in Southeast Asia. They looked defeated, moving doggedly about their work, heads down. Hopeless.

Dien! Damn him!

* * * * * * *

I went home and wrote my article, though I kept thinking about Dien all the while. It was a good article, too, and I'm glad, for it's probably the last one I'll ever do.

I have learned a lot of things since I got out of his dirty hands. Not only about fear and how to deal with it, but also about hatred. I could deal with him now, on terms that would give him a taste of the terror he had spent his life inflicting on others.

I hated a lot of the things it would entail. Leaving Dorothy on her own. Abandoning my work. But I had never thought I would have the chance to square things with Dien, and I could no more neglect this opportunity than I could erase the scars from my mind and my body. I knew I must attend to this monster as soon as I could manage it.

Tonight, if it is possible, I will do it. I am lying on my couch in the study. Dorothy is sound asleep in the bedroom. I can feel strength inside myself. I am no longer starved and abused almost to the point of death. Strange as it may seem, I am not even bitter, now that the time has come. I feel like an avenging angel of sorts.

All day, I have been thinking about the way in which to attack Dien. I know him too well to think that he is not well guarded; some of those slaves of his will be patrolling his land. I know all too well. I could never reach him physically. So I will get to him *non*-physically.

Closing my eyes, I retrace the route to his house, crossing the miles separating Cane Creek from my southeast Houston suburb. A dark tendril of hatred is reaching, reaching toward him, and I somehow feel that he is tugging it toward his sleeping body as strongly as I am pushing it.

Does something inside him feel guilty? Is some part of his consciousness—or his subconscious—needing expiation for the horrors he committed in the name of war?

* * * * * * *

I am relaxed now. My body is without pain for the first time in years. I am a black focus of rage, all aimed at Dien, asleep in that distant farmhouse. I know what is happening, but my mind is no longer controlling it. The hatred has taken charge, and I follow it with some strange disembodied vision, anxious to know what will happen.

I can see the house from above, like a negative of an aerial photograph. I see through the roof, into the room where he sleeps alone in a narrow bed.

The boil of rage that carries me along is focused into a single purpose now. We plummet through the intangible roof into that room. We hang above the bed, looking down on the sleeping face of Dien.

He moans and moves uneasily in his sleep. That smooth face is furrowed with a deep frown. Can he feel this black fog hanging over him? I hope so.

There is no hurry now. We are here, and there is time to appreciate the subtle cruelty of the hatred to which I have given birth. It is going to infect his dreams...and then what? I am anxious to know the depth of my own inhumanity. Am I as cruel, in my own way, as Dien?

Slowly, the cloud condenses, moving downward toward the man on the bed. We sink through his ribcage as easily as we did through the roof of the house. It is dark there, but his organs are outlined in glimmering nimbuses of phosphorescence. The lungs pump slowly; arteries surge with the burden of his blood.

That heart is trapped within the cage of his ribs, just as I was trapped for so many months in that bamboo cage at Quang-yi. It speeds its beating, as if feeling the approach of danger. We surround it gently, not touching it at first. We let it feel the chill of our presence.

Then we begin to squeeze.

Removed as I am, I feel the anguish that envelops my physical body, far away on the couch in my study. My own heart is struggling, crushed by pressures too great to bear. For an instant, my hatred lapses into fear.

So that is the price? Then it is a price that I must pay.

The rage swells again, pressing upon Dien's laboring heart, crushing it slowly and with infinite deliberateness. All that pain! I know too well how it feels, for in my distant body my own heart is dying.

Now I add a conscious effort to that of my black rage. We squeeze desperately, for I must finish Dien before I am overtaken by my own death. There is nothing in all the universe except pain. Such agony! It makes what I endured in that bamboo cage seem trivial.

Dien knows he is dying, but he cannot wake. He is terrified, but he can't cry out or move.

Hatred and death have locked us into a closer embrace than love could ever manage to do. I see into him, just as his sleeping mind sees into me. We understand each other fully, at this final moment, and neither of us is as good or as evil as we thought.

I manage a final convulsion of effort. It is enough.

* * * * * * *

From *THE HOUSTON CHRONICLE*, July 10, 1986:

SLEEP-DEATH CLAIMS
VIETNAMESE REFUGEE

HOUSTON—Nguyen Tran Dinh, 47, of Cane Creek has become the tenth in a series of unexplained deaths among members of the Vietnamese refugee groups living in the U.S. Coroner Stan Sublett, of Cane Creek, pronounced him dead at his home at six A.M., July 9, after he was found by his wife, Suyin, when she went in to awaken him.

Though Nguyen had complained of nightmares for some time, he had no known physical ailment. Heart failure is listed as the cause of death.

He is survived by his wife, Suyin, two sons, Tran and Ngo, and his parents, who remain in Vietnam. Private interment will take place in Cane Creek, later this week, under the auspices of Sublett Funeral Home.

* * * * * * *

Obituary Column, *THE HOUSTON POST*, July 11, 1986:

DRAKE, Harold Larkin—Interment will be at ten o'clock A.M. today at Drake Cemetery in Shelby County, Texas, for Harold L. Drake, formerly of 112 Live Oak Street, Deer Park. Mr. Drake is survived by his widow, Dorothy Elliston Drake, two brothers, Jonathan and Samuel, four nephews, and two nieces.

In lieu of flowers, the family requests donations to the Heart Fund.

We tend to be a lazy species and to try our best to make that easy. But automation carries its own potential for nasty situations.

A SNAP OF THE FINGERS

"I need a bit more light here," Sarah said, her tone rather apologetic. She felt a twinge of embarrassment again, but the salesman had assured her that she would get over that. And the company's brochure had explained in psychological terms why owners of their revolutionary furnishings initially felt foolish when speaking to tables and chairs and lamps. That was why they had invented the finger-snap code, which Sarah found eminently sensible, though she had not yet mastered it.

The lamp table shivered slightly. The bulb in the gooseneck fitting blazed into light, and the table itself waddled three and a half steps closer to the armchair where she sat.

Now Sarah could see the fine print, as she reread the contract on her new possessions. The guarantee, for all the tiny type, was iron-clad. Everything from the self-making bed to the self-setting table and the automatic kitchen set-up was solidly backed by the company. And what better arrangement could be found for a woman living alone, working hard at a demanding new job, and with a mother who tended to drop in unexpectedly to inspect her housekeeping?

She folded the contract carefully and slid it into the envelope. "Safe!" she barked, noting with satisfaction the authority in her tone.

An ornamental side table scooted forward, opening a polished door to reveal a sturdy metal panel fitted with a combination dial. "Four-oh-eight-two," Sarah commanded.

The dial spun obediently, and the second door opened. She put the contract inside beside her insurance papers, her car title, and the cash she kept for emergencies.

When the safe had returned to its place, she looked around her brand new apartment at her spanking new furniture. It all looked perfectly normal, no matter what computerized features might be inside them. Even her Holovision set was concealed behind a tapestry screen.

It was almost time for the evening news, and she glanced up at the screen. A tapestry eye was looking back at her, and as soon as it perceived that she was waiting for the set, it blinked out of sight. The tapestry rolled back, and the HV brightened to life. What a life!

All her mother's fussing and scrubbing and inspecting of feet before entering the house had been wasted, she saw. Why bother, when the Clean-U-Self carpet, the Auto-Scrub floor, and the No-Dust furnishings would do it all for you? She wondered why everyone didn't buy the stuff and throw away the stolid and unimaginative things they had been putting up with for so long.

It wasn't cheap, true, but the saving on cleaning aids alone would amortize it in just a few years. Not to mention the labor saved, particularly if you had to hire a maid. She slipped off her sandal and patted a bare foot on the deep-piled carpet, which all but purred at her touch. She shivered with a pleasure that seemed almost erotic.

The HV hummed to life, and the news moved in three dimensions before her eyes. When she winced at something gruesome or distressing, the set obediently blanked itself out until that segment was finished. Then it winked on again.

Bedtime found her wondering what came next. What new wonders would this new home reveal to her? The bed looked quite normal, the covers turned back to reveal a pleasant set of pale blue sheets and pillowcases. She removed her silken nightgown, which her mother had bought for her though she kept insisting she preferred sleeping nude. The sheets slid down to admit her, and they were cool and caressing upon her skin.

"Lights out!" she said, and the overhead fixture dimmed to nothing.

The prisms surrounding the fixture glowed. Interesting...her eyes focused upon the spinning balls of light, and she sank into sleep...into a dream that outdid anything she had ever experienced with any man she knew. She moved sensuously, and the coverings, the bed itself conformed to her body, stimulated nerves here, soothed them there. She woke full of vigor, pleased with the world.

From that day, her life became absorbing. She had never been outstanding at anything, and college had been a lot of work and study. Once her degree was in hand, she slipped quietly into her position, where she worked hard and was paid well, but in which she was only a cog in a wheel. She was what they wanted, competent and industrious and completely without ambition. She knew and always had known that she would remain in place until she retired—or died.

But now, for the first time in all her life, she felt superior. Her days at work were bolstered by her memories of the evenings at home, and now the antics of her fellow employees amused instead of irritating her. Her nights—ah, her nights had become something entirely out of the ordinary. It no longer troubled her that she had the reputation for being a loner, and few men still approached her for dates. She no longer needed men anyway.

Her mother's visit interrupted the quiet flow of her days. She'd known Mom would come, as soon as she was able to travel after her heel-spur surgery. That was as unavoidable as taxes (though her desk had solved a lot of tax problems for her. She wished it could solve mother problems as well).

She truly loved her mother. Though they had the usual conflicts as she grew up, she knew that she would have remained nearer her home if her job had not been here on the opposite coast. But she would not ever go back, now that she had a new and satisfying existence, and she hoped her mother would take her word for that without further explanation.

Mom entered the new apartment with her eagle eye peeled for dust or disorder. One speck of grit or fluff would have stood out as if spotlighted by her searching gaze, but Sarah had talked earnestly with the furniture the night before. Every inch was spotless, tidy, polished, scrubbed, and/or flawless. Mom sank into the armchair and stared around.

"Dearie, I have never seen a neater place. Can you afford a maid?" she asked.

"My new things do it, Mom. They are self-cleaning, self-adjusting, self-repairing. Everything does itself. I want to get you a full set for the old house—Pop will love it, and since your surgery you don't need to work so hard. You can read or go to garden club meetings instead of cleaning."

Mom frowned. "At my age, Sarah, I need to think I'm needed, even if I'm not. So I scrub a bit too much...it's good exercise. And your Papa would think I was sick if I didn't make him clean his shoes twice when he comes in. No, this is fine and dandy for a young person like you, with a life to live and friends and suitors coming and going. Not for me. Leave me my illusions a little longer, I ask you as a favor."

She smiled, and Sarah knew she meant it. She could see her point, but her comment about friends and suitors made her uneasy. If

Mom knew about this introverted and self-contained life, she'd flip her wig.

Mom stayed a week, and it took her one day to learn that Sarah's social life was nonexistent. It took her two more days to come up with Carl. She had old college chums in every city in the United States, and of course there was one in town with a son of suitable age and eligibility.

Strangely, Carl was strong, sensuous, employed, and was instantly attracted to Sarah. Suddenly, the erotic dreams, which she had thought were the most life could offer, were not enough. In fact they became distasteful, and she disconnected the mechanisms of the bed to stop its stimulation. She began sleeping in her bed and living for those hours every evening that she spent with Carl.

Sarah's mother, satisfied that the affair would run its course better without her supervision, took the bus home to Papa. She exuded confidence that she would return soon to a wedding. Sarah kissed her goodbye and turned to gaze, starry-eyed, into Carl's face.

* * * * * * *

Again strangely, Carl was old-fashioned and refused to visit her alone in her apartment before they were married. "I don't trust myself," he told her. "And this is too special to risk spoiling it by getting into a hurry."

Two months after they met, Carl carried Sarah over her own threshold, while Mom and Pop and his own parents stood in the hall and threw rice. Then, being good parents, they turned on their heels and took themselves away.

"You are going to love my furniture!" Sarah smiled up at her new husband as he set her onto her feet and stood looking around the living room. "There is never any housework. You will come home to a meal all cooked and a clean house and a wife who isn't tired to death after her own day at work."

She tucked her head into his shoulder. "And I will come home to a husband! That is the best thing of all."

They kissed deeply and moved into the bedroom. Behind them, the bed stirred uneasily. The drawers of the dresser slid open and shut with little gasps. The bedside table gaped its doors, then closed them silently. The shining balls of prism under the light fixture spun madly.

"Whoa. Let's catch our breath," said Carl, coming up for air. "I need a shower. We need to put away our things. And then...then we'll try out that luxurious-looking bed."

Sarah giggled as they stepped back. "Right," she said.

They didn't take long. And when Sarah snapped her fingers in the one-two code for lights out, the fixture dimmed with provoking slowness. The glass balls went still, and in the darkness the dresser sidled away from the wall, its cushioned feet silent on the carpet.

There came a soft bump at the door, which opened enough to admit the lamp table, trailing its unplugged cord behind it like a tail. But Sarah was unconscious of it all. Only Carl existed at that moment.

Only when he gasped, above her, and lurched away did she realize that something was wrong. "Something poked my back!" he said.

"Lights on!" snapped Sarah's fingers, but no light appeared. Something snaked around her neck, pulling her away from Carl and out of the bed.

"Urrgh!" she gurgled, struggling with loops of something that felt like electrical cord. She could hear Carl moving desperately too, and she managed to twist her head to see.

Even in the darkness she could tell that something was crawling over her husband—something soft and wide and dark and plushy... the carpet? That affectionate living room carpet?

She tried to scream, but the cord was too tight about her throat. Her hands were going limp, falling away as they tried to pull it free. Carl! Carl!

She struggled to turn, to see him...and he was no longer moving.

Something sounded hear her ear, a mere breath of sound. Words? Surely not!

"Traitor!"

And that was the last thing she heard.

With in-laws like these, who needs enemies?

CLAIR DE LUNE

The melody drifted through her sleep, haunting Margaret with memories of moonlight, of Arthur, of the place where they had been so happy. Debussy had been one of their common loves, and Arthur had brought her a tape recording of *Clair de Lune* the night he asked her to marry him. She had played the cassette for the first time on the small machine he brought to their tryst in the churchyard.

She felt the music in her bones, even as she dreamed. Sitting on the marble bench beneath the angel tomb, they had held hands as the clear notes purled through the jasmine-scented night, and she had known they would be together forever.

Or had thought she had known.

Margaret moaned and turned in her sleep, trying to recapture that moment of pure bliss. But, as dreams always do, the joy turned dark, and the jasmine scent was mixed with that of funeral lilies.

A metallic clang woke her, and she shivered. Now it was winter, not spring. Now she was alone and Arthur lay in the big marble tomb with his ancestors, not too far from the angel that had watched their love begin, and seventy-nine paces precisely from the garden fence beyond her window.

Another clang woke her fully, and she sat, pulling on her woolen robe and fur slippers. Shutters often banged as the wind rose, but this sound was more like metal against metal. She shook her head to clear her thoughts.

Their lawn abutted the old churchyard, without a fence of its own. Perhaps the wind had loosened the ancient latch of the side gate they had so often used. She went to the window and looked out into the night; milky moonlight drifted across the lawn, interrupted by patterns of cloud shadow. The wind was rising quickly, and the banging of the gate increased in volume.

There would be no sleep unless she secured it, that was certain. Mrs. Ames now leased her house, allowing her to retain the bedroom and sitting room she and Arthur had shared for such a short time. The old woman was crotchety, quick to anger. If she waked, there would be unpleasantness, and Margaret dreaded that.

Since Arthur died, there had been too much of it in her life. First the funeral, meeting for the first time those cousins Arthur had disliked and dreaded. They were exactly as he had described them, elderly crows, clad in rusty black, their eyes sharp and predatory as they gazed at the woman who inherited the house they coveted. She had refused their offers to buy it from her.

Family property—she could all but see the thought in their minds, as they drank the last of Grandfather Bisson's cognac. Not a word of sympathy had any of them offered her, and she had seen them depart with great relief.

There would be no help or comfort there, so she had turned to Arthur's second cousin Royal for help in planning her future. Roy had grown up with Arthur and knew Margaret would have a struggle to live on her inheritance, now that Arthur's accounting income was no more. He found a buyer, but again she refused to sell.

He had found Mrs. Ames. Though the tenant was unpleasant and difficult to please, Margaret blessed her for the lease money, which was substantial.

Shivering again, Margaret crept down the curving stairway toward the side entry. Alone in the dimness, lit only by the night light in the garden, she felt orphaned, bereft, almost frightened, though there could be no danger in this quiet and well guarded enclave.

Mrs. Ames thought differently, of course. She knew every superstition, every rumor of evil-doing, every villain ever hatched in the place, Margaret had found. Her store of terrible tales even included some about the Bissons, pillars of respectability though the family had always been.

As she closed the door behind her, Margaret sighed. "Oh, Arthur, if you had only known how hard it would be, surely you wouldn't have risked yourself on that wet road at night," she murmured. "We had so little time...."

The gate gave a vicious clang, as a gust swept the shrubbery almost flat and pushed Margaret toward the front walk. She did not resist, but hurried toward the church. She had to go all the way around the churchyard to reach the small gate that gave access to the graveyard.

The street lamps were far apart; pools of shadow engulfed her as she moved. The church was dark, even the lamp in the sanctuary unlit. She slipped along its stone side and approached the noisy gate. Its lacy arch of ironwork provided the anvil against which the loose latch hammered; she caught the swinging gate and pushed it into place, forcing the latch into its proper socket.

She did not turn at once toward her bed. Instead she stood, her hand on the curving ironwork, remembering. The cemetery had been their refuge, after the engagement was announced. Arthur's brother Lenville made the family home so unpleasant for the two that the cemetery seemed positively cheerful by contrast.

Only after Arthur asserted his rights as heir to the Bisson house and took control of his part of the family money did Lenville leave in a huff. He had never returned. She wondered how much of his share of the money was left. He had always been a spendthrift, Arthur had told her.

She pushed against the gate, making sure the latch was secure. As she looked up, a drift of moonlight moved over the pale stones; she thought she saw something there. A familiar shape...she shuddered with sudden dread. It could not be Arthur, though the square shoulders and the shape of the head were painfully familiar.

Arthur slept peacefully among his kin. Only the troubled dead walked, Mrs. Ames had told her.

"Mar-ga-ret...," came a quiet call on the wind.

"No. I do not believe. That is not Arthur but some night-born delusion," she said aloud. Now she did turn and ran toward her home.

"Mar-ga-ret...." The call was louder, with an edge of desperation.

She did not turn back. At the side entry she found the door locked against her. Surely she had left it on the latch! She had brought no key. Had Mrs. Ames waked and locked the door? She hammered against the solid panel, but there was no sound inside.

Margaret set her chin, which Arthur had admitted was firm and determined. There was a public telephone beyond the church; she would call the old woman and get her to open the door. But no...she had no coins. What could she do?

I will call the emergency number, she thought. That is free, and this is surely an emergency. The police will wake Mrs. Ames, and she will let me in.

She fled back up the sidewalk toward the church, forgetting for a moment the terror of that call she had heard. But the receiver was broken, and there was no dial tone.

Her teeth chattering, Margaret considered what to do. Arthur's old neighbors were gone. The great houses along the Avenue now contained businesses. There was no one nearer than the shopping center, two miles up the street. At this time of night, there might be no help available. Muggers and worse haunted the parking area at night.

Sobbing now, she moved to the side gate and sagged against it. In the churchyard she had known the happiest and saddest times of her life. It was, in a cold way, familiar and homelike.

She lifted the latch, and the gate creaked open. She felt her way among the stones to the tall angel and the bench where Arthur had proposed to her. She would be safe there, she felt, if there was any safety to be had on this strangest of nights.

The moon slipped behind a dark mass of cloud, and the gravestones disappeared in the dimness. Margaret huddled her knees to her chest, her feet up on the bench, trying to keep warm. She wouldn't freeze, of course, for southern winter nights were seldom that cold. She had her warm woolen robe and her fur slippers. But her hands and face were chilled, and she curled into a ball like a hedgehog.

The touch on her shoulder almost stopped her heart. She gasped for breath before she opened her eyes. The moon was visible again, and above her loomed the familiar silhouette she had never thought to see again.

"Arthur?" she quavered. "You're not dead!"

Then the moon glared out brightly as the cloud passed, and she could see the face clearly. "Lenville?" she asked. "How did you know I needed help...."

The pale face did not change. Hands grabbed her and pulled her upright. "You are a difficult woman," her husband's brother said. "I tried to get you to come in before, but you wouldn't. However, Mrs. Ames was on duty and locked the door. We might have had a problem getting rid of you, otherwise."

Understanding jolted her. "You are working with your cousins!" she said with complete certainty. "You got Royal to find Mrs. Ames to help you—but why? There isn't enough money to make it worth their while, or yours, for that matter. WHY, Lenville?"

His face darkened as the clouds returned. "The treasure!" he said in an impatient tone. "I'm sure Arthur told you about it; that's why you refused to sell when Roy found a buyer. We had to get you out so we could search."

Margaret shook her head. "Treasure? You must be joking! Arthur never mentioned any. And if there were and I knew, why would I rent out my house?"

He seemed not to hear; she recognized with horror the obsession she had seen in his eyes in that brief glimpse.

She looked past him. Four dark shapes appeared on the walk. The shadow of the angel touched them as they came toward her.

"We will put her in the mausoleum with her beloved Arthur," said Cousin Benjamin. "Nobody here knows her. If anyone asks, we will say she was irrational with grief and may have killed herself. I think Royal may be her only confidant. When enough time has passed, we will search desperately for her and...find her. Then we'll inherit what should have been ours before." He giggled.

Lenville nodded. Together the men lifted and carried her past the angel tomb. Borne aloft by strong hands, she moved toward the Bisson mausoleum, which hadn't even an angel to lend her comfort.

The door grated open. A musty odor wafted outward, and Margaret almost gagged. Mortality, no matter how well embalmed, has its own distinctive scent.

The wide doorway was built for carrying in coffins, so four men carrying an uncoffined woman didn't crowd it. Once inside, Margaret was dumped onto a slab that waited for some future Bisson who would never come. Then they stood staring down at her in the glare of a flashlight.

Blinded, she could not see them, though she felt their inimical presence.

"Now we come into our own," said Lenville Bisson. "We will search the house from top to bottom, and we will find the treasure our grandfather possessed, telling only his oldest son its hiding place. Father told only Arthur. But we will locate it, however long it takes.

"No one will ever know what caused you to hide in the tomb with your dead husband until you died. We will locate you, of course, after it is too late, and your death will revert the property to the family again, as the will ordered."

The light went out; five shadowy shapes loomed in the doorway and passed. The heavy door grated once again, and Margaret could hear the snick of the lock.

Stunned by the suddenness with which her life had ended, she sat in the darkness. Where was Arthur's coffin? She wondered. He had been placed very near the last empty niche. One—two—the third coffin to the right of it, she was sure. If she must die, it would be as near as she could get to her husband.

She felt her way, counting coffins. At the third she stopped and felt it over, searching for the bronze plate on which his name was engraved. That was the right one. Had her luck changed? She almost giggled at the thought, then caught herself. Hysteria would not serve her.

She lay on top of the coffin, her arms stretched about it. "Arthur," she murmured, "you have already died. Surely it isn't so very hard to do. Be there when I die too, will you?"

She sighed and closed her eyes. Then she opened them again, for she could hear Arthur's voice, in her mind or in reality...she could not decide which. "Open Father's coffin," it said. "Open Father's coffin."

Margaret turned and set her feet on the invisible floor. Which was that? Not the next. That was Grandmother Bisson's. The next was Grandfather's. But the next had to be Octavius Bisson's, for Roy had pointed it out to her when Arthur was entombed.

She found the plate, scrubbed away the dust with the edge of her robe, and felt of the letters. Yes. O and script and B and script. It had to be the correct one. But how did you open a coffin that had been sealed for decades?

Sighing, she felt for the catches. They were damp, encrusted with something nasty, but at last she managed to snap the first one open. Then she set her stubborn jaw and gripped the lid with trembling fingers. Using all her strength and more, borrowed from some unknown source, she lifted with all her might.

There came a whoosh, as if air escaped. The smell, however, was no worse than it had been before, so she lifted the lid clear. This was one of the old style coffins with one-piece tops, so she let that slide down behind the box.

The thing was open. "What now, Arthur?" she asked.

Again she found the answer, though she had no idea where it came from. "Feel under his feet. No one would ever think to search there."

The coffin was lined with silk, though now it was fouled with stuff she did not want to identify. She pushed the stiff ankles aside and slid her fingers under the lining. A sharp edge caught a nail, and she slowed, feeling her way cautiously.

There was a rectangular box, quite flat and thin, its edges almost as sharp as blades, beneath the coffin lining. She worked it out without disturbing the body, though she felt like apologizing to her unknown father-in-law as she laid the box on the floor and recovered the coffin.

The box was easy to open, which was a relief. Inside she found oiled silk enfolding a parchment-like document, a letter or a deed or a certificate, she thought. Could this possibly be the treasure that obsessed the Bisson kindred?

The container was thin and sharp and strong. Use a box as a tool to dig out? It seemed ridiculous, but that was all she had. Laying the wrapped parchment carefully on Arthur's coffin, Margaret took the box to the back of the tomb. In her ramblings with Arthur she had seen the mausoleums from all angles. The back of this one had some loose stones along its base, though it was likely no one else had ever noticed that.

She felt around all the blocks forming the rear wall of the mausoleum. Near the bottom row, there was a draft of air from outside, cold with the winter wind. Margaret chipped away at the line of mortar with her providential box, and chips and bits began to fall away. When she had dug out a line of mortar, the block shifted downward, and she broke loose the stuff holding its sides. After the first, the work was easier, though she was sweating with effort.

Before she freed herself, Margaret could see pewter-colored light beginning to glimmer beyond the wall. Dawn arrived as she crawled out of the tomb, holding a rolled parchment in one grubby and blood-streaked hand.

The janitor would arrive soon to open the church. Until he came, she would find no help, so she returned to the bench beneath the angel and unrolled the document in her hand. It was stiff with age but strong.

The thing was a letter, she was sure, but the script was difficult to decipher, written in Latin, she thought. The signature at the bottom took her breath, however. ER in an ornate script. Wasn't that the way Queen Elizabeth the First signed documents? She couldn't remember, for she was exhausted, dirty, and angry.

The janitor's cheerful whistle rang across the churchyard. Margaret rose and went toward the gate, hearing in her mind the delicate strains of *Clair de Lune*. Arthur had been there for her, even in death, she felt certain.

She would punish those who locked her in the tomb, but first she would put this precious item, whatever it was, into the hands of her favorite librarian. Anna would guard it to the death.

Then Margaret would do some haunting of her own, and her brother-in-law and his cousins would regret the day they decided to get rid of her. She would see them in prison, before she was done.

"Elton!" she called to the janitor.

He turned and stopped, shocked at her appearance, but she waved him toward her. "Hurry, Elton! Call the police. Someone... tried to kill me!" And that, she thought, was no more than the simple truth. She limped after his running shape, seeing the light grow brighter and hearing the last notes of *Clair de Lune* echo in her memory.

This one is just plain mean!

COLD DAY IN HELL

The chill was creeping through the room, though the old radiator clanked and fizzed determinedly. I kept wriggling my toes in my battered shoes to keep the numbness at bay. My portfolio was made of the sort of plastic that looks like leather, and I huddled it to my bosom to create a little warmth between it and my body. The ash-blonde secretary was made of such chilly stuff that nothing could have frozen her, and my timid request for more heat elicited only a raised eyebrow.

Time went as slowly as if it, too, had frozen. I wondered more than once why I bothered to wait. Mr. Tait Braithwaite had made it quite clear, once before, that he had no time for indigent but talented artists. Only the bright-eyed darlings of the arty set need apply. He hadn't exactly said it in words, but his meaning was clear. Though his own surroundings spoke of anything but affluence, his attitude implied that eccentricity was a prerogative of the influential. I had been properly quashed.

Why had he sent for me? The secretary, if she knew at all, wasn't saying. My own speculations did me no good. Only the fact that my tiny room was even colder than this dingy office kept me here, I finally admitted to myself.

Only that and the bitter realization that I had to admit, finally and for all time, that I was, as my father had said so many times, neither talented nor responsible enough to make it on my own, even in a relatively small city. Going home defeated would end me.

The clock on the wall by the door to the office seemed to have frozen, along with everything else in town. The minute hand crept round imperceptibly. When I watched, it didn't move at all. When I didn't watch, it made small forward movements that stopped immediately when my eyes turned its way. What seemed like hours snailed by.

When the intercom buzzed, I woke from a frozen and nightmarish brown study. The cool voice said, "Mr. Braithwaite will see you now." She indicated the door beside the clock, and I noted with astonishment that it said seven-thirty.

I opened the door and went in, still bemused by the time. I had come in at three. Surely no secretary would stay so late. Surely no sane clock would say four-thirty at one moment and seven-thirty the next. Surely....

But that fruity voice that I had disliked when first I heard it was saying, "Ah, Miss Thorne. You wished to see me?"

Now that was too much! The wait and the cold and the clock and the secretary had combined to put me in a bad temper, anyway. This was entirely the last straw.

"YOU wished to see ME!" I snapped. "I've waited for hours in your tomb of an office with your mummy of a secretary, freezing myself into an absolute corpse, and you don't even remember that you called my landlady and said for me to be sure to be here by three this afternoon. That you had a commission for me. I wouldn't have come otherwise, I assure you."

His wide mouth stretched to unreal proportions as he grinned at me. "I do like to see a pretty girl in a temper," he said patronizingly. "Makes 'em even prettier! But you are absolutely correct, Miss Thorne—may I call you Josie?—I recall now that I did want to see you, and I do have a job for you. A mite unusual, you could say. Out of the way as to time and place. A...highly unconventional subject...."

I interrupted him. "I made it clear from the start that I do not do porn. Not for the mass market, not for the private perverts. None at all!"

"No, no, no! Never pornography, my dear Josie. Simply a little job that will take a few hours. Unusual circumstances. I thought of you because you have a nice little talent, you need the work, and you aren't so successful that you'd turn down something a bit *outré*. That's all. A client of mine—very wealthy, highly eccentric—has lost a loved one. Unfortunately, she did not like photographs and never had any made. In the present circumstances, a new one would obviously NOT give the desired effect.

"He simply wants a pastel portrait of his sister, you understand, that makes it appear to have been drawn from life, not from... hmmm...death, so to speak."

"Oh," I said. I had never seen a corpse except that of my grandmother, when I was ten. Now at twenty, I wasn't sure that I wanted to see another. I still had an odd feeling about the rouge on Granny's wrinkled face, knowing how she had abhorred make-up all her strait-laced life.

"Miss Arpels will take you out in my car—it's only about twenty miles. She will stay until you have finished, then she'll take you safely home. Mr. Inverness will probably not appear at all. He is, you can imagine, distraught over the death of his sister—his only relation in the world. So sad. His wife went three years ago. Have I left anything out? Oh, the fee. He said he'd pay three hundred dollars for an excellent likeness, two hundred for a merely good one, and one for an adequate one. As well as my commission. Generous. So do a good job, Josie. This could be the beginning of things for you."

Though the thought of twenty miles in the company with the icy Miss Arpels chilled me even further than I was, I nodded. I was in no position to turn down anything halfway respectable. And three hundred dollars would keep me for a month. With a few commissions from Mr. Braithwaite, plus, perhaps, more through recommendations from satisfied clients, I just might make it.

As Mr. Braithwaite had provided easel, paper, and pastels, I had no need to return to my home for my own. Even my portfolio proved no problem, for Miss Arpels locked it in a cabinet in the office, to be retrieved later. So, sooner than I would have wished, I found myself in a garnet-colored Lincoln, being driven through the snow much too fast by a blonde who now seemed the literal incarnation of the Snow Maiden. Though I will admit that the Lincoln made up in comfort for the office's lack.

I slept, after a while, for the darkness hid any scenery that might have slid by as we purred along. When I woke, we were pulling into a curving drive that ended at the dark bulk of a house. Only one light was visible under the wide portico, but another popped on as we pulled to a stop.

A well-dressed man with the air of a servant took my case of equipment and led us into the hallway beyond the wide door. I almost took to my heels, then and there, for the house was filled with almost tangible gloom. When I looked directly at the wainscoted walls or the decorated arch of the ceiling, there was nothing wrong with either. But just on the edge of vision a sort of darkness seemed to intrude.

Still, I buckled up my nerve and followed the man into what must have been a drawing room in happier times. It should, indeed, have been full of gloom, for it was draped in dark blue velvet, floor to ceiling, and in its middle was a bier with the body of Miss Inverness on it, covered with a white lace pall.

Strange to say, the room was full of a sort of tingling anticipation. It puzzled me, all the time I was removing my coat, chafing my hands to life, and setting up the easel. At that point, I almost dropped the whole thing, then and there, for the body began to sit up. A hasty word from Miss Arpels calmed me, and I saw that the bier had been made so as to lift upward like a hospital bed.

"Mr. Inverness felt that you could get a better likeness if she were in a sitting position; you know how the face seems to sink in on the bones, even in the living," she said.

I gulped and nodded, though my insides were still quaking from the shock.

The manservant, whose name was not mentioned, moved to the side of the bier and lifted the veiling from the body. I moved the lamps, so as to light the face in as lifelike a manner as possible, but when I looked into the dead face I was startled. She didn't really look dead at all. Certainly not the stiff, made-up sort of dead that was my only yardstick.

She had been, I could see, beautiful in her youth. Even now, at what must have been fifty or more, she retained a fine-boned distinction. Living, she would still have had enough color to make her lovely.

As I lined out the composition and drew in the preliminary lines, I felt a surge of interest at the challenge of this first commission. Few in my calling, I guessed, had begun their professional lives in such a strange way. And as I worked, I became more and more interested in my subject as a person.

"Why did she never marry?" I asked Miss Arpels, who sat beneath a lamp, reading a *Vogue* with a bored air.

"Oh, she married. I don't know who, and I don't know what the family did about it, but she was back home and Miss Inverness again before anyone had really missed her. Probably a fortune-hunter conned her." Miss Arpels went back to *Vogue*.

I had never before become so engrossed in my work that I needed no intervals to stretch my muscles or relieve my eyes. Something in the tingling air of the room, with its faint trace of sandalwood, seemed to buoy me up, as the face on the rough paper before me waked into life.

The clock on the mantel was bonging midnight when I looked up from the portrait, stood, and stretched widely. "She's done," I said to Miss Arpels.

But when I turned, she was no longer in her chair. Instead, there was an elderly man, thin and gaunt and gray, who looked piercingly at me, then at the portrait. He smiled then, and I felt that three hundred dollars was going to be the price.

His smile grew wider and wider. His hand came up from his lap, and there was a carved stick in it that he moved as a conductor moves his wand. The tingle in the air grew so electrifying that I seemed to be quivering inside my skin. Shaking loose from myself....

The room wavered and grew misty, and I felt my mind and spirit being wrenched free of my body. When I could see again, I saw the room from an odd angle, and the man was looking down at me. Shocked, I saw my own familiar face, my own tall slender body in its old plaid skirt and brown sweater. It was standing there, animated by someone who was not I.

I tried to open my mouth. Then I remembered that I had painted the mouth quietly closed, with a hint of a smile. I cut my eyesight as far to my right as possible, and the face on the bier was just within range. It was dead now. Truly, inarguably dead.

Inverness said, "It will be a cold day in Hell before anybody suspects anything happened here. I'll adopt you as my *protégée*, my dear sister, and you'll move here with me. Then you can unobtrusively give up your career to take care of a sorrowing old man.

"You have a new start! And when Braithwaite finds one to my liking, so will I. We can live the lives our parents refused to let us live."

"And she?" asked the voice that was and was not mine. "She will be a nice little portrait and never open her mouth," he answered. "She is trapped there by my spell, able to think, able, perhaps, to feel, but quite, quite helpless."

And so I am as I am, a human spirit confined in a body formed of pastel on paper. But nothing can stop me from thinking and plotting and contriving. Even bereft of hands, there is something I can do, if I will it hard enough. What one person's willing can do, another one's can undo.

A cold day may come into Hell before anybody expects it.

Another mean little tale. I live very near Cajun country and have spent some time in Louisiana. The Cajun culture is not one we understand very well.

DEVIL-CLAW SWAMP

Armand was panting hard by the time he reached the edge of the forest bordering the swamp. He kept reassuring himself that it was his exertions, not panic, that were exhausting him, but he knew, deep inside, that it was the pursuing swarm of angry Bontêtes that compelled him forward.

Armed with shotguns older by decades than Armand, rifles that had, some of them, seen action at the Battle of Vicksburg, and guided by dogs that could sniff out a coon or a possum or a polecat with unerring ease, the family intended to get their revenge at last. The white lightning that old Ernest supplied to fuel their enthusiasm would carry them far and deep, and the young man knew that he would do well to hide himself completely, if he intended to see another dawn.

He plunged into the thickets, remembering, even after so many years, the feel of the deep leaf-mold under his shoes. The yeasty smell of the swamp came even here, and he turned toward the maze of creeks and sinkholes and many-kneed cypresses that could hide an army, if its leader knew the way into its depths.

No matter how long a swamp trapper had been gone, he would always recall the ways he had taken, every morning of his young life, to run his lines. Between the mink and muskrat and coon caught in his steel traps and the catfish in his nets, he had managed to get himself all the way through the Beaufait school system. He did not intend, even as a child, to stay in this country, ignorant and poor and tied to a houseful of brats and a whining woman.

He took a deer trail that led in the right direction. It wasn't the one he had used ten years ago, but nothing in the swamp ever stayed the same. The pools, the creeks, the sinky-holes all changed location from time to time, and he would have to go on intuition as much as memory, if he was to find a safe hiding place deep in Devil-Claw Swamp.

He should never have returned to Beaufait, not even for the bit of property his father left him. Only Papa, of all the Villefois clan, had stood by him after Annie drowned. Papa might have suspected him of holding the girl's head under, when the pirogue overturned, but if so he understood the reason. A shotgun wedding would have kept Armand tethered to the swamp country. The thought had made him go mad with desperation, when she told him a baby was on its way.

Nobody else knew, of course. That was why the inquest found that Annie died by accident. That was why his cousin Nora cried when he took the train for Chicago, using the bit of money Papa had saved for emergencies. But Ernest Bontête suspected. He had been livid when the inquest came out as it did. He had fixed Armand with his good blue eye and his blind white eye and cursed him long and thoroughly. "You come back to this country," he said in his voice that echoed the gallons of raw 'shine that had gone down his throat, "I kill you for sure. You hear that, Villefois? My family, we come after you if you come back again to Beaufait."

So he had not come, though Papa had fallen sick, after a few years, and hinted in the letters that Nora wrote for him that he would like to see his son again. The last letter had been too pitiful. Papa was dying, Nora added at its end. If he was to see him again, he must come at once.

He should have known better! The bus had dropped him off outside Beaufait at the gas station, and he had walked down the dusty track to the house that had been his home. The garden spot that Papa always kept green to bursting with growing things was a plot of ragged weeds. The house needed paint.

Worst of all, Nora met him at the door, her eyes cold and shuttered against all the memories of their shared childhood. "Your Papa, he is dead. The Bontêtes know you will come for this house, the little land, the tiny money he save for you. They expect you, Armand. You go for the woods, right now—they will be looking already. Someone was to watch the bus for you."

She handed out Papa's wood-cutting boots, his thick denim jacket, and the .22 that always stood beside the door for shooting water moccasins or bobcats that bothered the chickens. Armand sat in the splint-bottomed chair and changed his thin-soled city shoes, lacing the boots with shaking hands.

He was remembering—not the civilized city ways that had veneered over his old ones, but the reality of life in this swamp country. The Yankees had it all wrong. It was not high drama, the feuding. Not heroics. It was simple and businesslike, a killing for a killing.

He could hear the dogs belling before he got across Papa's big field. He found himself glad of the boots—they should mix the scents, anyway. He angled toward the big creek and waded along its autumn-shallow flow until it looped widely eastward. There it was joined by a cut that held a trickle of water, and he followed that until he could find a tree whose branches swooped low enough to reach and strong enough to hold his weight.

Once he was aloft, he squirreled from tree to tree, thankful for the heavy limbs and the thick foliage of the stand of water-oak in which he found himself. When he dropped to the ground again and headed for the swamp, the dogs' high-pitched voices were far behind him, traveling at an angle to his direction.

He had hunted and trapped and fished in Devil-Claw all his life, following his Papa there before he was old enough to go alone. Though it had provided all the cash money he had possessed for years, he hated and feared it, then and forever. Now he caught a whiff of remembered stinks, heard the edges of wavering calls of water birds, the bellow of a gator, the mournful hooting of a conclave of owls, getting ready for their evening hunts.

Armand held himself in check, watching his steps, brushing out prints in the dusty track with handfuls of weed, holding himself to a steady pace. Haste would get him caught. Getting caught would get him killed. He had to stay calm. As the ground softened underfoot, he recognized the small streams that began to meander about his route. An ancient willow that he had used to mark his trail, years ago, had fallen, but its snaggled stump still was standing.

He held to the right of it, finding the narrow strip of firm ground that he had prayed would still be there. It led off into the waterways, a dependable pathway into the maze of the swamp.

Though it had been bright when he crossed the last clear patch, the sun was less than two hours from setting. In the tangle of big cypresses and brush, it was all but dark. He should, he thought, have grabbed Papa's lantern from its peg, even if it might have delayed him for a few seconds.

Moccasins would be crawling, in the dark, and anyplace where he could hide might well contain a copperhead or a coral snake. The gators would stay put in the water or on the mud banks, but snakes were a real danger.

He wormed forward into the swamp, hoping that no super-smart dog would nose out his trail. Many a hungry boy, among his schoolmates, had tried to trace his path to his traps, when he was a child. Nobody else had managed it, as far as he knew. Traps that were sprung usually held their prey. Lines left baitless were infrequent. No, he felt sure that nobody had ever studied out his route into Devil's Claw, in the years that he was gone.

Ten years of floods and wildfire and occasional drought had changed his old way. There was water where he expected firm land at times, though he always managed to find the track again. Trees were down—a tornado had ripped through, he decided, changing the entire look of the country. He kept going, feeling his way now, never relying on his old memories too much.

At last he came to a nest of trees that some giant seemed to have jerked from the ground and dropped in a jackstraw tangle. Huge trunks angled upward, their crowns interlocked. That tangle looked solid enough to hold a man, even if he fell asleep, he thought. He checked his trail for tracks, swept out any possible traces, and climbed the handiest of the tree trunks, making his way cautiously upward, watching for snakes all the way, even though there was little light left to see by.

He made himself a fairly secure place to rest, and, as he settled into it, the pale gray of the last twilight faded into blackness. Nothing moved near him except for a few late mosquitoes. From time to time a firefly flashed its spark off among the trees, and a gator slapped his tail against the water, at some distance. There were owls enough in the swamp, he felt sure, to have a convention.

He was shivering with the dampness of sweat, the cool of the fall night, and the reaction from his flight. His leg muscles jerked and quivered, and he found that his teeth were chattering. With a terrific effort, he pulled himself together and went still.

He heard hounds. They were distant, but they seemed to be coming toward him.

Armand cursed softly. Why had he messed with Annie Bontête? Why, having messed with her, hadn't he resigned himself to marrying her and living as his people had done for a century? Why hadn't he stayed in Chicago, secure in his job and his apartment and his unsatisfying but safe girlfriends? Papa was no longer alive to help him out of this situation. None of his kin, not even Nora, would lift a hand to help him.

It might not have been so bad to be married to Annie. She was quiet and loving and easy to get along with. He had never wondered if that baby was his, and now he found himself thinking of the sort of child it might have grown up to be.

Ten years old, it would be...Armand sighed and shook his head hard. It did no good to think of such things. Annie was dead, with the child, and he had killed her. Her grandfather was perfectly right in that. Those dogs coming across the creeks and the fields would find him, if his luck ran out—but not if he could help it!

He huddled his arms around his knees. The damp was getting into his bones, and around him squawks and screeches and the croaking and peeping of a million frogs filled the night so that he could hear nothing else. But through it all, even as he tried to blank out the noise, came a cry from deep in the swamp.

He held his breath, his ears straining. It came again, bringing back sharply to mind the evening he had run his traps and heard that awful sound. He had tried to forget it, and he had forgotten until this moment. Through the third cry he heard the voices of the dogs, much closer now.

Armand squirmed higher into the tangle. From two directions, the sounds drew nearer. Devil-Claw Swamp—Papa had told him that the devil was much stronger in the town than in the swamp, but Armand had somehow known better.

His eyes were adjusting to the gloom, the streaks of phosphorescence giving him something on which to focus. His ears were straining to hear, and that was why he detected the regular "swash! swash!" of steps moving through the water, before his gaze caught the first of the bits of rotten wood, glowing as they curved on the disturbed water beneath the treetops where he cowered. Something big was wading, out there, getting closer, calling more loudly.

The .22—Armand checked the chamber. Empty. Nora had not reloaded it, as Papa always did after shooting a chicken hawk or a possum in the henhouse. He gripped the gun, his hands going numb.

Behind, where he had come in on the trail, he heard a low growl. One of the hounds was there! He couldn't see it, but he heard it drawing breath to give its first baying call to the rest of the pack. His guts cramped as he waited.

The howl came from the other direction, long and harsh and full of sadness and misery. The hound gave a stifled yelp and pattered away, back up the track. Armand ignored it, straining his eyes to see what came glimmering through the swamp, knee-deep in the black water.

Now it seemed to be singing...that funny little song he had learned in Miss Treville's first grade class. Devils didn't sing!

The shape was faintly phosphorescent, patches of darkness outlined with filaments of greenish light. It was tall, broad, terrible. The hands moved at its sides, holding back button-willow or trailing vines. As it moved beneath the treetops, the face turned up toward Armand.

"Annie!" he moaned, leaning forward, forward, until he fell into the muck at the creature's feet.

The gator, which had been waiting patiently for something large and luscious to come its way, lashed its horny tail, stopping his struggle to get his face above water. With a sinuous motion, the reptile moved into position and ended the game with one many-toothed bite.

The creature, its singing stopped, its voice temporarily silent, stared down at the bloody remnants at its feet. Then it turned its own face, which was certainly not that of any woman living or dead, toward a promising channel, and continued its nightly stroll.

*Catfish weighing hundreds of pounds have been caught in the
Atchafalaya River. What if they began catching people?*

FISH STORY

Tolliver was dynamiting all the time, day and night. His son-in-law, the road engineer, used his explosives permit carelessly, and he
let Sam have all he wanted.

Those living on the bounty of the swamp and the river, the
streams and the fishing holes began to suffer because of that, for
Tolliver dynamited for fish. There was no hole so deep, no stream so
hidden that he could not find it at last and blow its denizens to King-dom Come with his blasts.

Small victims of his explosions were left to rot on the banks of
streams or ridges in the swamp. Alligators died of the impact and
were picked by buzzards and their wallows were left uncleared, so
that the swamp began drying out, very slowly.

Yet those who lived on the water and understood such things
could see the result. The balance of nature was being upset, and be-cause of that the Felicia Swamps were disappearing, bit by bit, as
the fish became fewer. The D'Urbervilles, who lived in a stilt-legged house on a hidden bayou beyond Maum Felicia Lake, were
affected first and worst. The catches in their nets dwindled so rap-idly that the long-headed sons and the arthritic Papa told it all up
and down the country that their fishing grounds were being ruined.

Their small purchases of coffee and cigarettes all but ceased, as
they had no fish to sell for cash. Their wormy children began look-ing like starved chickens. That was why Arnaud, the second-youngest D'Urberville, was out so late, scrounging around for a pos-sum or a coon to take home to his hungry family. The fishing had all
but ceased, and they had eaten their scraggly bantams down to the
last rooster, who was too tough even to boil to broth. He had taken
his skinny hound into his pirogue and was poling it along a bayou

very far from his usual haunts, when he first noticed something strange.

Ordinarily, just about sundown in the swamp there was an ear-splitting chorus made up of the voices of early frogs and owls and bobcats and late hawks and jaybirds and wild pigs. Mourning doves and screech owls and bull gators raised their various calls and cries, until anyone who didn't know where he was would have thought he'd strayed into an African jungle.

But this evening, as the twilight gathered under the mournful cypresses, it was still. Still as death. Only a single sound, the slap of a gator-tail on water, went off like a pistol-shot as Arnaud held his pole quiet in the water and stared at old Vine. The hound stared back as if he was as puzzled as his master, and both of them shivered.

But the man had to find something to take home, or Emilie would have him by the ears. She wanted her children fed, and the roots and vegetables she managed to scratch out of the muddy bit of soil she used as a garden only whetted their appetites.

He waited for a while, as it grew darker under the trees and the water swirled around his pole. But nothing more stirred except the light breeze in the high reaches of the cypresses, and he knew he must go on. Vine raised his head and turned his nose into the breeze. His right ear went up, and Arnaud knew that he had scented game.

"Go, Dog!" he said, his tone soft as if to keep from interrupting the stillness. "Get 'im!"

Vine was over the side in an instant, leaping to a nearby log and from that to the more solid ground to the east of the channel they followed. Strangely enough, he did not begin his usual hollow baying. He simply made off at top speed across the treacherous ground, crossing open water by swimming and leaping over anything that looked like quicksand.

Arnaud, in the pirogue, had to go the long way around. Without the hound's voice to guide him, he was soon confused as to which direction was the one in which he should go, though he knew that if Vine went east to begin with, then east was it. He had only to keep bearing that way, when the channels would allow it, and sooner or later he would find Vine or the dog would find him.

He sighed and began poling again, along a murky tributary that seemed to go in the direction he wanted. But he heard nothing—not even the quick patter of Vine's paws on the leaves and mud. And still no night-bird began its calling, no panther screamed, no owl swept overhead on velvet-soft wings.

That was why the blast almost frightened him out of his shoes. The world seemed to shake to its roots. Cypress needles scattered downward, along with loose bark and dead branches. He sat suddenly in the bottom of the pirogue and caught his breath.

Tolliver! The damned lawbreaker couldn't even let a man hunt for an animal for food without messing things up!

At that moment, a terrible thought came into the mind of Arnaud D'Urberville. He knew, for once, just where to find Samuel Tolliver. He would be there, off to the left, which was roughly northward. He would be gathering up his prizes in the big eddy that cut into the western bank of Rive Saint Félice. That was, if he reckoned rightly, not more than three miles distant. And the main channels all ran in that direction, toward the river.

It would be easy to hunt Tolliver. That would not feed the small ones tonight, but perhaps, if he managed to rid the swamp of the dynamiter, it would mean that there would be fish later on.

Abandoning Vine to his hunt, Arnaud turned the bow of the pirogue downstream and followed the sluggish flow of the creek. It would end at the river, he knew, and he had only to keep from grounding or from ripping out the bottom of his boat on a cypress knee.

The long rifle lying along the bottom of the boat was loaded, as always. In the swamp, a hunter never got more than one chance at his mark. One shot would be all he needed, for he was a notable marksman, and Tolliver would be a much larger target than a coon or a possum or a chicken-stealing bobcat.

He pushed along more quickly than was quite sensible, but something drove him toward his goal. He had lived too long under the shadow of this bad man. It was time he did something positive. He emerged into the river in a shallow bend a half mile below the eddy that he felt certain had been Tolliver's target for the night. Indeed, in the moonlight that now silvered the sinuous channel of the Saint Félice, he could see pale glints of fish bellies floating downstream. Shoals of them. Thousands of them. All food for his children, but wasted and left to rot on their way to the Gulf of Mexico.

He drew a shaky breath and poled his pirogue into a shallow spot along the bank. Pulling it out of the water, he hid it in a clump of bushes. He checked the load of his rifle, felt his shirt pocket for extra rounds, and set off on foot along the bank toward the eddy above.

Even as he went, he stepped softly, scarcely daring to break that unnatural silence that still gripped the night. But even at that, he went fast, and in half an hour he stood staring across the deep bend that helped to form the eddy. Tolliver's big boat was anchored just downstream, and the man had nets stretched along floats to catch what was still floating up from the depths.

The man himself was a dark shape against the silver ripples beyond his craft. He moved with sureness, never hurrying, never slowing, as he checked the nets, threw back the fish that were of no use to him or hauled aboard (sometimes with a winch) the big sixty and eighty-pound catfish that were his trademark.

Arnaud's breath went out of him in a trembling sigh. He had come to do murder, a thing that his father and mother would abhor. But, should he succeed, he would never tell a soul. Only his conscience would be troubled by that guilt, and the children would eat again. Perhaps, even, they might have something sweet, from time to time, when the fish sold well.

He checked the damp ground behind a log for snakes. Then he lay at full length and trained the long rifle over it, aiming at the dark shape working busily with the nets.

Yet, even as his finger began to tighten on the trigger, something made him pause. There was a sound. A water-sound. He had thought he knew them all, but this was new to him, and it somehow filled him with dread. He turned to look downstream, toward the deep river where catfish had been caught that were true Leviathans of two and three hundred pounds.

A pale glimmer of water was moving upstream—the bow-wave of a boat. But no! There was no boat.

He peered through the moonlight and water-glint toward the disturbance. Something huge and rounded was pushing along beneath the water, and that frill of wave was the point at which its shaft-like fin broke the surface.

He squinted. Perhaps it was his imagination, but he thought that he could see a swirl of disturbance where a tremendous tail propelled that great body forward.

He sank behind the log, risking just his eyes over its protection. Whatever this was, he did not want to come to its attention. And then he thought of the man on the boat. Tolliver was standing still, when he looked again. He seemed to be staring toward that oncoming shape, although it was too far, really, to be certain of that. The boat was still, the nets unchecked, the winch silent.

D'Urberville held his breath, as the great catfish head broke the surface just aft the fishing boat. The moon shone on the wet skin, and even at that distance the watching man could see that the whiskers beside the grinning mouth were like cables or snakes, thick and dark.

The great body curled along the side of the boat, and the vessel began to rock. A shout echoed over the water and from the wall of trees beyond it. The small dark figure seemed to be clinging to the rail. But the rocking went on, and the water about that spot grew creamy with turbulence.

Arnaud heard a dull crunch. Had the catfish bitten into the hull? Or had a log come down the river at just that moment? Never, afterward, could he be sure what actually happened, but the boat began sinking quickly. It was the instinct of all his kind to go to the aid of any fisherman in trouble. Even now, even knowing who this one was, it was hard not to try to help him, but Arnaud held himself still and quiet behind his log.

Tolliver had damaged the swamp and the river. He had earned the wrath of all its denizens, human and other. Whatever happened now, it was his just due.

The struggling black shape pitched forward, as the boat went down. A grinning mouth was waiting for him, and it closed to silence his screams. A tail-fin moved strongly, and the big cat disappeared from view, leaving the river quiet, rippling, undisturbed except for its dwindling burden of dead fish.

D'Urberville lay for a long moment, staring out over the eddy. Around him, birds began tuning up, their tones tentative at first. A long cry from the swamp was answered from across the river. An owl swept past, its downy wings silent in the warm dampness of the air.

Far back the way he had come, Arnaud could hear Vine's excited voice, trailing something. He stood and took his rifle under his arm. Oblivious to noise, he rushed down to his boat and pulled out far enough to gather in a bounty of fish—catfish, perch, eels.

Among the floating debris, he gathered in something dark, lumpy. It was only when he unloaded his catch at his own rickety pier that his father saw what he had picked up with his trove.

"By damn, Arnaud, this be a foot! A foot in a boot! How you get dis, hey?"

The young man grinned in the lantern-light. He had been saved from murder by something too strange and huge to understand. It was safe to say, now.

"Tolliver's foot, Papa. He go down in his bateau, and a catfish eat him. We take it to town tomorrow, eh? Get him a pretty big funeral—everybody go and drink and say how good he be, and his wife, she smile behind her veil.

"An' we—we go back to fish pretty good, now that nobody dynamite, any more." And he pushed out of his mind forever the memory of that vision in the moonlight.

Few, in this modern era, have any idea of the power of ancient artifacts. We collect them, display them—what if we had to live with the consequences of them?

THE GIFT

"You know I don't like such things. Go without me, dear." Even as she spoke, Helen knew her sister wasn't really paying attention. The girl was holding up her costume, examining her reflection critically. Nothing but her Gypsy dress could find a spot in her mind, Helen knew.

She tried again, touching her shoulder. "I don't know the Raymonds—they're your friends. I never liked parties, especially masquerade parties, the silliness and the costumes and the noise. Do go without me, Maura. You'll be with Jonathan. It isn't as if you must go alone."

Maura whirled, making the bright layers of skirt swirl about her. "You're alone too much. Reading! Writing! Brooding and morosing!"

Helen laughed helplessly. Her sister could always crack her up with her invented words. "I live alone just so I can do all that reading and writing and morosing without interruption. I like all the things you never did like. Why can't you believe it? And now you have your husband persuaded he must help you 'get me out of myself.' What nonsense! Only when I'm at work am I truly 'in myself.'"

Helen did not mention the particular thing that disturbed her, among many about this party. The Raymonds had just received an inheritance of ancient artifacts their uncle had managed to pilfer from one of the digs he helped to conduct. Though well-qualified as an archaeologist, the man had been very slack as to ethics. It was the thought of such precious artifacts in private hands that disturbed her.

She didn't particularly like the Raymonds anyway. Their new wealth had gone to their heads. Their very old house had been renovated, ruining the very things that had made it historically valuable. The depredations of the renovator were either ridiculous or hideous. Better never to have been wealthy at all than to be that sort of *nouveau riche*.

She said nothing to her sister, however. Maura took everyone at his own evaluation. To have been invited to this festivity delighted her, for she was a shameless social climber. Now she turned to Helen with her "I'm a poor orphan child—be good to me" expression. It had always worked in getting her way with Helen, and it didn't fail now.

* * * * * * *

Being for adults only, the party began at nine. At a quarter after eight, Helen checked herself in her mirror. Though she hated dressing up in any form, she had to admit that she looked stunning in her black velvet gown, the only formal thing she owned. It was cut medieval style; she had added a rope of pearls to her thick braid of inky hair and a wide golden belt that tied in a knot and dropped a pair of ornate tassels down the front of the skirt. If she called herself Mary Stuart, she didn't think anyone at the function would know enough history to object.

It was unusual for her to own anything so formal, but it had been purchased for a reading of her poetry on the occasion of winning the Pratt Award and had hung uselessly in her closet ever since. She had not agreed to go to such an occasion afterward, though she had won more prestigious and rewarding literary prizes since.

The touch of the velvet brought back the reading in one detailed flash. She hated that gift of hers when it made itself known in such ways. Reliving her—and sometimes other people's—past could be frightening.

Maura and Jonathan arrived just in time to walk with her, two blocks to the Raymonds'. To arrive in costume, cramped into their ancient VW, would be ridiculous.

The autumn night was warm, but a brisk wind was ruffling the leaves along the gutters. The moon, almost at the full, winked above the whipping branches of oaks and elms. A perfect night.... Helen recalled trick-or-treating with her small sister in years long past. They had roamed the dim streets safely then. Now only the fact that they were three adults kept them from being at risk.

The Raymond house stood in the center of a huge lot—at least five acres—surrounded by a formal garden studded with oaks and hickories, beneath which Indians had probably camped when they were saplings. Their porch was lighted with a row of Chinese lanterns, and the double doors were open. A motley crew of costumed figures occupied the wide entry-hall, which in southern fashion had been turned into a living-room.

Maura and Jonathan (both as Gypsies) were lost almost at once in the crowd. Helen found herself in the clutches of Elissa Raymond, who squealed like a teenager and led her about the rooms on the first floor, introducing her to the guests. Helen realized at once the real reason why Maura and Jonathan had been invited, though she responded as gracefully as she could manage to people impressed at meeting the winner of the country's foremost prize for literature.

"You simply must meet our local poetess" (the term grated on Helen almost unbearably). "She has won all sorts of literary prizes, and her books are being taught in colleges!"

The uncomprehending but awe-stricken responses made her uncomfortable. Poets were evidently very strange beasts indeed to Elissa's peers.

"We particularly wanted you to be here," her hostess gushed, "because tonight we intent to unveil Uncle Stanley's collection. You have written about such things, and we felt it would be interesting to you. You can probably tell us such fascinating stories about them."

"I have studied archaeology a bit," Helen admitted. "But I'm no expert. I really feel that such artifacts should be in museums, where true scholars can study them."

The subtle dig didn't penetrate Elissa's veneer. She piloted Helen round and round until she felt like some sort of ocean liner in the grip of a particularly determined tugboat. The appearance of refreshments gave her a chance to catch her breath and to have a moment with Maura.

The younger woman was starry-eyed. "The girl with the red hair and the elf costume that almost isn't there at all?" she whispered. "That's a starlet! And all the local bigwigs are here, too. Mr. Prentice from the bank and Doctor Chadwick and even Representative Hallock. I never thought I'd be asked something like this, Helen. Thank you so much for coming—I think they asked Jon and me just so we'd bring you."

Helen found herself almost reconciled to her own discomfort. It was seldom, nowadays, that she could do something to make Maura happy. Jon took care of that most efficiently.

All too soon, the tables and trays were cleared away. The Raymonds took their places; it was obvious an announcement was on its way. Elissa cleared her throat, and the babble of talk died away. "Tonight we have a special treat for all of you. It's particularly appropriate that it's Hallowe'en, because these things were found in a tomb!

"To make it even more interesting, we have with us Helen Woodheath, whose works of poetry and prose have been concerned to a large extent with such ancient treasures. I hope she will...."—The woman glanced sideways at Helen and giggled girlishly—"...write a poem about tonight."

Sidney Raymond gestured up the wide stairway. "We have the artifacts displayed in the blue bedroom, just upstairs. If you'll follow us, you will be able to file through in a double line. Do take all the time you want and ask anything you like—we may not be able to answer you, but Miss Woodheath might."

Helen sighed and took her place beside the couple as they ascended the steps. She hated things like that! Then she forgot her immediate reaction as a wave of...something poured down from the room at the top of the stairs.

She felt almost sick. The gift! This was the sort of situation that brought it out fully! She clasped her hands hard over the knot of her gold belt, holding her quivering stomach in order with both hands and will power.

The host and hostess conducted her through the blue bedroom first, as she might have to answer questions about the contents. She found herself staring in amazement at a long table filled with svelte figurines, some with two heads, some with none; rings and bracelets and necklaces of obscure gemstones and mother-of-pearl were arranged artfully on velvet and satin.

The sense of antiquity was almost as tangible as smoke, obscuring her vision. She felt dizzy and reached out to brace herself against the table. Her hand touched something cool.

She jerked it back, but Elissa was already saying, "That is the one we intend to give to the museum, but we would like for you to wear it tonight, just to please us. Then you can give it to whichever institution you think would get the most out of it."

Helen stared down at a necklace made of green and blue apatite beads. A single strand made a loop large enough to slip over the head. From the sides of that, two loops of the linked beads fell, to be caught up together at the center of the bottom loop. At that point, there was a polished disc of mother-of-pearl, which shone with many colors in the subtly controlled lamplight.

It was beautifully made, its design sophisticated—and she recognized it. Others like it had been found at Catal Huyuk, in Anatolia. She had been reading about the excavations there since the conclusions based on them had begun to find print. The oldest human city found, so far. She shivered.

"I really can't take the responsibility...," she began, but Elissa held up her hand.

"Nonsense! We insist!" she said. "Besides, what could possibly happen to it here in this lovely little town, surrounded by your friends and neighbors?"

Your friends and neighbors! Helen thought, but she said nothing. She was caught, but she felt an unexplainable reluctance to touch the cool stones, to slip the loop over her crowned hair and about her throat.

The low-cut neck of the gown allowed the stones to touch her skin. She could feel the weight of the mother-of-pearl pendant below her collarbone. The room began a familiar blurring, shifting—she forced herself to focus on her hostess.

Elissa led her to one side of the room, and people began to come in. There seemed to be too many of them, more than there had been downstairs. And they looked odd.

Helen felt the weight of the necklace, heavier than before. She seemed to see red gleams of firelight. The walls of the room looked different—surely the wallpaper hadn't had such garish pictures on it!

A shape stopped in front of her—did it wear a costume with crow-like wings? She peered closely, telling herself it was only a dark cloak. She smiled, with some difficulty, and answered a trivial query about one of the statuettes of the Mother Goddess.

"Yes, this was found at Hacilar." The sound of the word made her dizzy.

Time crawled, and she felt disoriented and dreamy. Again, the room changed. The people changed. The faces changed. She closed her eyes hard.

When she opened them, she almost screamed. The walls were painted in strange patterns and colors. A fire burned on a brazier at one side, and rows of oddly clad people crouched on the floor like a flock of giant birds.

Where was the bed? The table? Now the small goddesses lay on a stone slab. An elaborate silver dagger, engraved down the blade with boats of some kind, lay near the edge.

Helen tried to turn, to look for Elissa, but she couldn't move. Something held her immobile, her head lifted, as if searching for something at the corner of the ceiling. She opened her mouth— perhaps if she shrieked, she could bring herself out of the grip of her gift. This had to be a result of the necklace she wore—but she had never before had such a strong sense of reality.

Instead of a scream, her lips formed a string of words. The language was strange to her, but she knew the meaning of the chant rising in her throat.

"Mother Goddess, we offer to you life for life, flesh for flesh, fertility for fertility. One stands here as offering, waiting for your presence. The Faithful wait, the priestesses wait. Outside, the men wait also, with the children.

"Make the soil fruitful. Send young into the bellies of the women and the animals. Send rain for our cisterns and our crops. We, who are your grateful children, await your presence."

Now she was silent. Those facing her stared, unblinking, entranced. There was a darkness near the ceiling now, descending slowly, shot with sparkles of light; tiny lightnings played in the midnight swirls. Those kneeling on the floor dropped their foreheads to the pavement beneath their knees. Only she watched the Goddess descending from her cloud.

Helen, terrified yet immobile, found herself thinking of many things. The shapes of winged angels. The robes tradition had put upon prophets and gods and priests. What she saw now was moving out of the cloud, a bright shape formed of wings of force, folds of light, a column that might be human-shaped but was most probably not.

Words entered her mind, couched again in a tongue she did not know but understood with some deep instinct. "It has been so long—and they send me a poet! How devout these late-sprung children of men have become! Their harvest will be superlative and their children many. How pleasing to my godhead is the life of a shaper of words!"

Helen found herself laughing. Hysterically. Not one of those in the room would know or care, until entirely too late, if crops failed entirely. Certainly none of them wanted more children—or any children at all. Almost every woman there would be appalled to find herself pregnant. The blessings of the Goddess were incomprehensible to them!

Now the winged shape was extending itself toward her, drawing her into its fiery folds. Words came into her mind, poetry of penetrating brilliance. Descriptions of places she had not seen with mortal eyes, of musics never heard by living ears.

From a great distance, she heard the sound of the necklace dropping from her dissolving neck onto the parquet floor. She heard shrieks and exclamations. She heard Maura's voice, tiny, faint, lost behind the moving cloud in which she was enveloped.

"Helen!"

But she was no longer Helen. She was dissolving, becoming a part of the living force that was the Goddess. Barely aware of the partygoers left staring at the spot where her living body had dissolved into the cloud that had absorbed it, she felt her atoms flow into the being of the goddess, her spirit become one with that infinite awareness.

They moved together, as a mist, as a brightness, through the intangible roof and into the face of the round-eyed moon. And Helen, at last, understood the most profound nature of her poetic art.

Often people think that I am a sweet little old lady, but I have a WICKED imagination!

GRIMM'S WAY

Ahead of him, the magpies began quarreling in the treetops. Behind, the very dust of his horse's hoofs swirled up into angry columns of grit, as if to pursue and subdue the rider who was the cause of their formation. Grimm did not notice, and if he had done he would have laughed.

Not that he laughed often. His reddish face and his burnished hair and beard blended together into a sort of wrathful sunset. Those who met him upon the road turned aside and picked imaginary stones from their steeds' hoofs or goaded their lazy oxen to get past him more swiftly. He did not invite the courtesies of the highroad.

Today he was in a hurry. The bailiff of a distant farm (inherited from his wife who had managed to die, being unable to turn aside from him or to spur past) had failed to deliver the rents upon the date when they were due. Grimm did not brook such failures. Floods? More like excuses. He'd make the fellow's ears sing when he arrived. And the backs of those tenants who lived by his whim would now smart to the tune of his whip, if they did not produce the necessary halving of their crops.

The horse's gait flagged, and he used his spurs impatiently. He bought only the best in horseflesh, and he expected only the highest in performance from his beasts. The struggling breaths of the animal aroused no pity in his heart. When Grimm hastened, suffering was the lot of any creature concerned in his haste.

Even so, it was almost dark when he arrived at his destination. Lamplight gilded the hoofs of the beast as he halted with a groan in the doorway of the bailiff's stone cottage. Through the open door Grimm bellowed, "Jakob! Come out to me!"

There was a long silence. Then a mutter of whispered talk. Then the sound of steps on the stone floor. Light steps. Dainty steps. Not those of Jakob's heavy feet.

The shape in the doorway was certainly not that of the heavy-set bailiff. A tall girl, slender as a birch, stood there with a lamp in her hand.

"My father cannot come. He lies within, folded into his winding-sheet. He drowned today in the floods while trying to rescue a small group of sheep that had taken refuge on a knoll amid the waters. If you wish, I shall go up to the House and light a fire for you. My mother will bring what food she can prepare at short notice, if you will be patient." The quiet voice held no doubt that any sane soul would have patience in such circumstances.

"Dead? Jakob? Nonsense! Stop this dilly-dally, Girl, and send him out to me!"

She lifted the lamp higher, and Grimm saw her face, pale now with grief but so lovely that it set his craggy heart to thumping in his chest. "My father serves a better Master now than he was blessed with in life. If you cannot believe my words, come into the cottage and see with your own eyes."

He was unused to such straight talk. Bemused, he dismounted and went into the low doorway, along the short hall, and into a tiny sleeping-chamber, where a corpse lay on the bed, surrounded by cheap tallow candles. A shadow on the other side of the bed moved, and Grimm saw that it was a woman whose very shape breathed grief like an odor.

He felt his color rising even higher in his face, but he thumped forward and touched the still face beneath the sheeting. It was cold as wax. Beneath his rough touch, the cloth slipped aside, and the sculpted visage beneath ignored him with an indifference that felt insulting. A better Master, indeed!

But there was nothing that he could do to punish Jakob for dying. He could, however, make life less comfortable for the wife and the daughter, and he proceeded to do so.

"Fires, at once, in the House. Call Wilhelm from the stables to take my beast. A hundred gulden, and he wheezes like an old woman after a day's hard riding! Food, as quickly as can be done! Move, the two of you! Do not think that Jakob's death frees you from my mastery!"

As he turned away he caught the full benefit of a glance from the girl. It would have curdled new milk—but the eyes from which it blazed were large and the darkest of blues, the shade of certain pansies after rainfall. Grimm shook himself and stalked away into the darkness to his own door, some yards up the lane of poplars.

Fires were lit, food brought, but not a word more passed the young woman's lips. Grimm found himself trying to provoke her to speech, even if it required the most brutally unfeeling of comments to do that. He felt unaccountably angry. More so than late rents and the death of a valuable servant should warrant. And when Grimm was angry, anyone caught within range of his tongue or his fist blanched and fled.

Except for the girl. Her name, if he recalled it rightly, was Truda. He kept calling her for trifling services, nagging at her because the damp kept the fires from burning well.

She seemed not to hear, beyond what was necessary to serve his wishes. The pale oval of her face was calm, indifferent as that of the corpse had been. There was no flicker of that blaze he had surprised in her back at the cottage. The more he tried to rouse her to anger, the more serene she seemed. It was unnatural. Even the men who served him quailed at such treatment, and his late wife had wrung her hands and twitched at her gown and worked her shriveled lips when he began it with her. She had run out of tears, much to his relief, long before she managed to twitch her way out of her life.

This woman treated him with the calm control that one used with a willful child. Not by so much as the compression of her lips did she take note of the cruelty of his words or the anger that was aimed directly at her head. The more he cut at her, the less she noticed him.

At last, worn out with both his long journey and his frustration at his lack of success, he took himself off to his unaired bed, where the old woman had put hot bricks to warm away the chill. That in itself fueled his wrath. He would have preferred that she forget, so that he could rake her skinless with his tongue for it.

The next day brought no relief. There had, indeed, been floods. Fully half the sheep had drowned, despite Jakob's efforts. Fields ready for harvesting were deep in water, the grain spoiled and bursting. There was nothing to be had there. Even he could not leave his tenants totally without sustenance, and there was little enough of that. His anger grew monumental.

He appointed another bailiff and took great pleasure in evicting Truda and her mother from the cottage. And when it came to his attention that the new and younger man had asked Truda to be his wife, thus securing the home still for her and her dam, that set fire to the oil of Grimm's spirit.

"Truda will come with me. My wife being dead, I need a woman to serve my needs. The old woman can warm your bed for you, if you insist upon it, but the girl goes back with me!" he shouted at the dumbfounded man.

There was nothing to be done but to go, and Truda packed her scanty belongings into a kerchief and mounted the pony he ordered up for her to ride. Not by the twitch of an eyelid could he tell her feelings in the matter. There were no tears, no lamentations at being parted from her only remaining parent, nor any for her separation from the man she had agreed to marry. The snowcapped mountain above the valley held more expression than her face, as they set out (at a more moderate pace than he had adopted before) for his great house in the next valley.

There was less cause for travelers to avoid his course on the return trip, but, after glancing at his face, they drew as far to the side of the road as was practical. The dust that swirled after the horse's heels took its usual forms—only to be broken up and blown away by the passage of the pony bearing Truda. The magpies quarreling ahead of them seemed more subdued than they had upon the outward journey. And Grimm noticed. He did not laugh.

It was dark when they reached the gates of the mansion he had gained with the hand of his wife. Torches burned in sconces on the tall stone arch, and they rode beneath in silence. He had determined at last that it was undignified to continue trying to elicit talk from the girl, so he, too, had fallen silent for the last half of the day.

Journey or no, he insisted that she serve him his food, pull off his boots, make ready his chamber for the night. As he watched her move smoothly about the room, his wrathful soul rejoiced. At last he would wring some response from her, of hatred or pain, if nothing more. He reached for her as she turned to leave the room, and she slipped between his fingers, as if she had been a wraith, ignoring the command he flung after her.

It was late, and he was weary. Too weary, he told himself, to trouble with pursuing her and bringing her back to his bed. Besides which, it was undignified for the master of the house to chase after wenches, however beautiful. He knew that his men would snicker after him, should they see what was happening. So he let her go for the time, but promised himself that she would suffer doubly when the time came for reckoning.

When he rose and went to find his morning meal, she was waiting, remote and cooperative as usual, to serve him. He did not know where she had slept, or how she had managed to find a clean gown, but she had done both, for her eyes were clear and unblurred with weariness. There was something else. In the hard morning light, she had a familiar look to her—it fretted at him as he ate and drank and cursed her.

There was much business to do, for his absence had left matters to wait his return. He turned his mind to other things, but he promised himself that the night would find matters far different from the last. That thought warmed him all the day, as he haggled and connived and cheated those he dealt with in his accustomed way.

After meat, that evening, he sent her to prepare his room. Following her there, he locked the door and set the key in a secret place while she was busied about her work. His temples throbbed with pressure as he waited for the moment to come. Whether lust or anger was uppermost in his mind he could not tell. But he was determined to make the girl suffer the consequences of all his frustrations for the past days, if she died of it. She would not be the first—or, by all that was holy, the last.

When she drifted past him, he caught her wrist in one huge hand. The door was immovable. She did not struggle, though he had hoped she would. She said nothing, as he dragged her toward the big bed whose canopy hid the rich coverings she had just turned back. She moved pliantly, without digging in her heels or making any unseemly commotion. Her face...damn her! Her face was calm as if she slept at her mother's breast.

He reached the bedside and turned her in his huge hands to face him. He shook her fiercely, but her head did not flop on her shoulders, her hair did not become disarranged. He might as well have shaken a wax image.

She was cool in his grasp. Not cold but remote, withdrawn, untroubled. He felt that nothing he could do, brutal—even fatal—could reach into the core of her being and open what was closed against him. She was immune to him!

The thought made him boil inside. His skull throbbed with the pressure of his wrath. He pushed her down onto the bed. She fell into a modest and graceful position and looked up at him serenely.

Her eyes were familiar. Even as he watched they changed from her darker eyes to Helga's cornflower-blue ones. The face...it, too, was changing. No longer young and smooth, it was wrinkling, reforming into a shape so well-known that his heart thudded thickly in his chest.

The faint scent of herbs that had always hung about his wife came to his nostrils. His hands seemed paralyzed, hanging at his sides.

The withered lips were moving, speaking. "I was afraid, in life, to thwart you in anything. Death removes all fears, did you ever guess that? You would have taken Jakob's daughter from her mother and her husband-to-be. I felt her tears, even in the grip of death as I was. And it came to me that this did not have to be. I could prevent it—I knew it without doubt. I took her shape, Grimm. I deceived you and her people. Even now she is celebrating her wedding plans. For you brought me with you all this way. You will have me with you for the rest of your life—it is what you deserve."

She laughed, a shrill grating cackle that had always set his nerves on edge.

His throat seemed to swell. His head pounded with the pressure of his anger. "No, Helga!" he shrieked. "I am rid of you!"

His fingers, freed of their paralysis, closed about the sagging throat. A terrible pain shot through his head, and his hands began to numb again. The candlelight was tinged with scarlet...black.

He loosened his grip, heaved upward to catch at the canopy. It pulled loose with the screech of tearing satin and fell after him as he dropped, quite dead, upon the empty bed.

Not all horror is supernatural. Too often, these days, it is techno-logical and meant only for the best.

INQUISITION

It isn't every prison that comes equipped with every possible convenience. In all my years of research into the Middle Ages, I found very few Inquisitors who seemed to be trying to help their victims, rather than to pry them loose from property or influence. My torturers are altruistic to a fault, I find, though that is no comfort.

While I read those crabbed manuscripts, all the spidery records and journals from centuries ago, it never occurred to me to wonder how it felt to be caught in the toils of the Inquisition. Secure in health and youth, I did not find it in me to put myself into the place of any long-dead victim. But now I know how it feels. Now I know.

Except for being sanitary and determinedly cheerful, this hospital could exchange places with a dungeon below some inquisitorial keep of old without shifting gears. The pain dealt out is identical, no matter whether it may or may not be intentional. And, unlike its forerunners, this torture chamber is extraordinarily expensive.

I have no way of telling anyone my feelings concerning the matter. I can't speak. I cannot hold a pencil to write, for a stroke felled me at a single blow, leaving nothing functional except my brain. I stare out through my eyes like a prisoner from a cell, hopeless and without any possibility of rescue.

Those who love me best, straining every nerve to anticipate my needs, cannot read in my gaze the demand I have tried to convey. And if they are unable to read me, how could a therapist or a nurse, who knows me not at all?

They manipulate the useless limbs attached to my log-like trunk, and I watch, the futility driving me to tears. I try not to look—those tears seem to distress them a great deal, and though they can't help me, I do try to help them, if only by trying not to worry them. It isn't their fault that they are torturers. The system has taught them to consider themselves healers and helpers.

With my own Rosa, it is worst of all. Now, unable to do anything to distract my thoughts, I begin to understand matters that never impinged upon me before. My wife, being a physician, is frantic and frustrated. All her skills are useless to help me, and she cannot even attend me formally. It is never wise for a spouse to treat her mate. I never understood before that the treatment would be identical, yet the provider of it would suffer too much while torturing the loved one. I had not grasped that.

The shots burn in my veins like liquid fire. I am moved and handled like a doll, while my damaged nerves do the shrieking that my lips cannot. When they turn me, I can see my wasted body, and the bones of back and sides scrape on the mattress. My arms lie, hard as sticks, across my ribcage, when someone folds them on my chest.

I bear this by shutting my mind off from the tangle of nerve and bone to which it is attached. This is not easy—it is hardly possible at all. But otherwise I would go insane, in my claustrophobia and desperation. I would kill myself, if I could move. A wrench to pull out the tube from my wrist would do it, if nobody came too soon. But it cannot be done. Nothing will move.

I have tried to will Rosa to inject air into the tube. That would be a safe way for her, as nurses constantly inject medication into the IV. I would die painlessly (I hope) of an embolism, and we all would be free of this horror.

But Rosa still has hope. I can see it in her eyes and in her actions, when she comes to sit at night. She thinks that things will be as they were, somehow, some time. Being a doctor has not removed her ability to dream. She brings our sons, when they can get away from jobs and families, and even the grandchildren lined up in the hall to wave to me, looking sad to see me so.

My body is, of course, dying by millimeters at a time. Painful fraction by painful fraction, it is escaping from my torturers and their intravenous medications and nourishments. Eventually I will go free, but I should not be asked to endure this terrible waiting for death to end my suffering. I am filled with shame that I have been guilty of trying to sentence others to such agony. The eyes should have told me what they endured, but I did not—would not!—see.

I have written articles opposing euthanasia, and medical journals, as well as popular publications, have printed them. When the bill to allow suffering terminal patients to die came up in Congress, I was totally involved in attempting to have it voted down. How ironic! If only I could let my people know my wishes, it would now save me from this agony.

Doctors I have not met come to poke and prod me, as if I were an exhibit on a morgue slab, already dead and unable to protest. They think my mind is gone, I can see, though it is more alert and clear than I can ever recall being before. But perhaps they find their tasks easier, if they think the sufferer is unable to feel or to know what they do.

Rosa, of course, does know. We stare at each other across a terrible distance, and our sons, too, come and talk quietly with me of their lives, trying to keep me involved. They still feel that I am the Dad who solved their woes when they were tiny, although our roles are reversed now. They dread finding me gone, and the fabric of their world irreparably torn.

But oh, how I want to go free! They will know, I fear, how much, some day, if they are as luckless as I have been. We all must travel the road to death, in one way or another.

Today Rosa came in smiling. "Harold is coming!" she said. "He has only just returned from Italy, and he called to find how you are. He will have news about his researches in the Vatican Archives."

She wiped my face with the damp washcloth, cleaned my hands, combed what was left of my hair, and went over the stubble on my chin with the electric razor. "Now you look like Doctor Frederick Harben," she said. "Ready to lecture!" She meant it. I could hear it in her tone—poor Rosa! Lying to herself.

I thought about Harold, as she puttered about the room. We had been friends for forty years or more, co-authoring several scholarly works in our mutual field. We understood each other as few human beings manage to do, mind speaking to mind almost without words.

Rosa bend over me and kissed me on the forehead. "Harold will be here soon. I must make my rounds—take care, Love."

Harold came a few minutes later. He laid a bunch of flowers on the table and came to stand beside me. I stared up, trying to convey my gladness through my gaze.

He had been braced for worse than he was seeing, I understood at once. I must look pretty good, after Rosa's efforts. I struggled frantically to make my recalcitrant flesh respond, even by as much as a grunt. Nothing happened, but Harold saw. He understood the effort I made, even though it produced no result.

Pulling a chair close, he touched the switch to raise my bed so that I could look into his face. He gently turned my head to make it easier, and that hurt, but not more than everything else did. I kept my eyes fixed on his, willing him to understand my meaning.

He closed his own eyes for a long moment. Then he reached to take my hand, holding it between both of his. That was surprising. I never recalled touching him for more than a handshake, in all our time together.

His hands were warm and steady, and something flowed to me out of him. A pulse of life almost revived hope, though we both knew it was impossible.

He laid my hand on the bed and looked into my eyes again. "I see, Frederick. Rosa is wrong; there is no hope, is there? You are in agony—it's there for anyone willing to see it."

I blinked three times, slowly and deliberately. It was all I could do.

"This stuff...."—he gestured toward the hanging bottle, the tube with its measured drips traveling to my wrist—"...is just holding you against your will. Trapped. Desperate...." There were tears in his eyes.

I blinked again, hard, squinching my eyelids together.

A nurse tapped on the door, coming with the regular shot, which she injected into the tube. In a moment, the fiery stuff flooded into my arm, and I closed my eyes again, tightening them against the pain.

"You can't confess, can you, Frederick?" Harold asked, his voice grim. "You can't say anything to get them to stop, for they don't know they are torturing you."

I stared up again, for he had risen to bend over the bed. He saw the pleading in my gaze, and he nodded. "I'll talk to Rosa. She is a sensible person, and once she stops seeing through her hopes, she will be able to see through your eyes. Because the new law is in place, it will stop, old friend. I will see to it."

The door hissed shut quietly, leaving me to think of his words. Only one person in all the world had heard my silent cry. Perhaps now it would end.

* * * * * * *

He managed to convince Rosa. She came in this evening, her eyes filled with tears, and bent to stare into my face for a long, long time. I blinked in measured rhythms, doing my best to convince her of the thing she did not want to know.

She took my hand and held it, as Harold had done, but her fingers quivered with protest and with pain. I blinked again.

The boys came, soon after, to say goodbye. The grandchildren were outside on the lawn, and Sean carried me to the window for one last look.

I am fortunate in my family. Once they understand, they do not hesitate or look back. I assume that they are now attending to the legalities of my situation, for Dr. Stern has come into my room. He is looking down at me, his face sad. I can feel his grief.

Now he is disconnecting the tubing. The needle pulls out of the vein, sticking a bit because of its long stay there.

"It may take some time," Stern says, his voice almost inaudible.

I blink three times, and he understands.

Now all I have to do is wait. The doors of the prison are beginning to open. The torturers have, at last, gone away.

You must remember that I am a sweet little old lady—at midnight on the last Tuesday of a leap year...maybe!

THE ORPHAN

My mother was eaten by wolves. I watched the whole process, hidden in that tight cranny in the rocks into which she had thrust me at the last moment. Even the dark night couldn't hide what went on from my terrified young gaze. Snow light provided more than enough illumination, and I couldn't manage to close my eyes. Not even when they rolled her over, and her almost fleshless face stared directly into mine.

A kind Providence sent heavy snowfall before they were done. Though I could hear the snapping and grating of teeth on bone, along with an occasional ominous cracking, it was far better than seeing what they did. And that snow must have hidden my own scent to some extent. That, or else the beasts were too full of Mother to scramble among the stones after me. As it was, they snuffled and grunted and growled about the spot until almost dawn. Then they left, shadowy in the white-on-white landscape.

I was, you must understand, no infant. That would have been as fatal as the wolves, in the circumstances in which I now found myself. No tiny child could have survived that night and found its way through the heavy forest, floundering in snow that was neck-deep in places. But I was a sturdy ten-year-old, tall and strong for my age. She had often remarked upon that.

So I struggled with death through a night and a day, and I came at last to a woodsman's home. Though it has become fashionable to refer to such dwellings as huts or hovels, Mischa's house was neither. And Mischa was no serf.

I have thought since that he must have been the eccentric son of some noble, choosing to live on the remote edge of a great family estate. His house would have been a good one, even in a town.

Though it was not large, it had no need to be, for he lived there alone. Still, it held comforts beyond my small imagination.

I found it by accident, literally knocking my head against it as I staggered, head-down, through a fresh fall of snow. That thump must have been loud enough to rouse Mischa from his winter torpor, for I fell upon the doorstep, too exhausted to cry out. When the door opened, I looked up and up and up into a pair of sparkling black eyes that seemed totally surrounded by a fierce black beard, black hair, black moustache. All curled rampantly about those eyes and a rather stubby nose with a hint of rosiness to it.

"What now?" rumbled that deep voice that was to become so familiar. "Who comes falling upon my door on such a morning?" He bent and lifted me as if I had been a hare.

The interior of the house seemed overly warm, after that night of dire cold. My face felt as if it might burst, though my hands and feet were quite numb. My impromptu host seemed to know what to do; he brought a small tub of cold water and laved my limbs until they tingled. Then he brought warmer water. It seemed as if icicles were growing outward through my flesh, but he soothed me and dried me and gave me, at last, a cup of tea so hot that I had to sip very slowly.

When I was able at last to be attentive, he set me on a settle piled with scarlet cushions and sat opposite me on a hassock. This brought our faces into some alignment, and he looked me over carefully.

I must admit that I did the same to him, but my first impression was never bettered.

He grunted, in time, and asked in as gentle a voice as his rumble would muster, "And what is yourr name, youngling? Where is yourr home? Who is yourr father?"

The last was a question I hated to be asked. I had asked it of my own mother until she had forbidden the issue. My grandfather seemed sad when my paternity was mentioned—sad and almost afraid. So I learned to keep my peace, though I knew that my name was Dmitri Petrovitch Orlov. My mother's had been Anna Grigorievna Spasleva.

"His name was Peter Orlov, I think," I answered, taking the last question first. "My mother would not talk of him. Grandfather shook his head and sighed when I asked of him. I think he must have died a long time ago."

"Verry likely." The giant put his bushy chin in his hand and looked at me even more closely. "And yourr motherr?"

"My mother is now a wolf. Or part of several wolves. They ate her, last night. You see, her father was Grigor Spaslev, of the village Bulenki. He died a week ago, and we were sent to my Uncle Dani. But the men took our money and left us alone in the forest to die." I glared into that bushy face. "I lived! And when I grow up I will hunt those men down and kill them." I'd made that resolution while I crouched amid the stones, listening to the crunch of Mother's bones.

His great laugh boomed until the loops of sausages danced against the ceiling of the kitchen. There was an inquiring snuffle, and a great boarhound crawled from beneath the settle and looked at him, then at me.

I should have been petrified with fear. He could have swallowed me with two snaps of his huge jaws. But he held up his nose, and I touched it with a tentative hand. We were friends, as simply as that, a matter that only death ended.

"So you are now an orrphan?" Mischa asked. "And I am alone herre in these grreat woods with none to talk with except Boris. Perrhaps you would like to live with me? I take it that none of yourr own will come looking?"

I shook my head. "Uncle Dani didn't truly want us. He has many children. But Mother was his sister, and he had to take us in. No, he will not look for us, I think."

So it was that I became Mischa's adopted son. I had longed for a father, there in the cramped town where every boy seemed to have one. Yet I had never dreamed of living in a vast forest, of learning to hunt and track wounded beasts, to read hints in the sky and the scents of the wood and the activities of birds and animals. Most of all, I had never dreamed of anyone as complex, as interesting as—frightening—as Mischa.

Nobody ever came near his house. Once or twice in the year, he went to the nearest town to buy things he might need. It took days to go and days to return, and he did it as seldom as possible.

There was no road nearby, not even a track. The soldiers of the Tsar did not come into the forest, for there was no one here but Mischa, and he troubled no one and had no money for taxes—at least I assumed so. I had thought the tax-gatherers came wherever there was money, however far and dangerous the road might be.

Not only did I learn woods-lore. Mischa could read! The fact stunned me. And he had books. That threw my theory about his lack of money into disarray, for books were matters only for the rich. Everyone knew that. Yet those books became my companions, for my foster father taught me to pronounce the letters, to form them into words. Suddenly the pages unlocked, and I found myself looking into far places that I had never dreamed of, or entering worlds that Mischa assured me existed only in the minds of the men who had written down their descriptions for others to marvel at.

My mind grew even faster than my body. I asked thousands of questions, many of which Mischa could answer. Now that I am an adult, I realize he must have seen some of the world outside Mother Russia. Perhaps he attended one of the great Universities that he spoke of. His mind was filled with many rich things.

Yet there were times when he answered no questions. He would grow surly and angry. Even Boris would slip quietly from his path at such times, and I learned to be seen and not heard. This did not happen often—it was at least a year after I came to him that I noticed it first.

Once I had experienced the moodiness, I realized that it came upon him only once a year. Usually it was in mid-winter, but occasionally in the summer. He would begin looking haggard and feverish. In about a week he would fling out of the house without a weapon. He would not return, sometimes, for three or four days. At such times, Boris would whimper and slink and seem terrified of him, though the dog adored his master otherwise.

As long as I was very young, these fits shook me more than I cared to admit, even to myself. As I matured, it came to me that it might be these very seizures that had sent Mischa to live in the forest. Without them, he might not have been where he was at the time I needed him most.

At last I grew old enough (and foolish enough) to indulge my curiosity about his actions during these times. When one is eighteen, few things are frightening and nothing can be allowed to be forbidden. One mid-winter day, when Mischa had gone into his yearly mystery, I donned my furs, took Boris and my gun (Mischa had bought it for me on his last trip into town), and followed his trail. I waited until he was well out of sight before beginning this rash venture, and once on his track I found he was traveling very fast. I had to use every bit of skill he taught me, just to make certain he did not elude me.

The forest was very thick. In these days, when so much of the timber has been taken to build cities for the Tsar, it is hard to make one realize how very thick the forests were then. Only natural fires or windstorms thinned the great trees in those days. And it was through one of those natural thin spots that Mischa had set his course. Young trees, bushes, fireweed made a tangle for miles, yet he kept to that rough way instead of turning aside into the untouched forest on either hand.

Even with the thick layer of snow, it was hard to keep to the trail. A time came when I stood and stared down at something I could not explain. His track—the right boot—was indented, clear and fair, in the deep snow. Then there was a scuffed spot. The track of a wolf went away from that.

One wolf. No single wolf, I knew in my heart, could match Mischa, yet he was not here. No man-track went away in any direction. I remembered the whispers I had heard at other boys' hearths in my childhood. Things that told of men who became wolves—or wolves who became men. My hair prickled on my neck. Boris sniffed at the wolf-track, howled once pitifully, and fled toward home.

I followed him, very slowly, very sorrowfully. For two days we waited for Mischa's return.

He came, as usual, at dawn. His face was drawn, his cloak full of burrs and tangles. He found us waiting for him, and he seemed to sense at once that something had changed, finally and forever.

"Do you become a wolf, Mischa?" I asked him, though I knew the answer.

His eyes filled with tears that spilled into his beard, where gray streaks now marked the black curls. He sat suddenly and wiped his mouth on his cloak, and I could see dark stains on the fur.

There came a deep sigh. I did not hurry him, but sat on the settle where he had put me so long before and looked across at his deep chair before the fire.

"So you, my little one, have seen? And you know my terrible secret, which drrives me into the haunts of beasts, forr I am not fit forr those of men!" The tears now flowed freely, glistening in his beard and dropping onto his hands.

"All those years ago—were you there when they ate Mother?" This was the burning question that had kept me wakeful all the days of his absence.

He took away his hands and looked into my eyes. His gaze was dark and sorrowful. "I may have eaten herr myself!" he shouted, covering his face again.

So I killed him. It was not difficult, for I remembered the method the grandmothers whispered about in the chimney-corners. He seemed glad to die, and we buried him, Boris and I, in the forest that he loved.

No person ever inquired for him. Not one living soul missed him, except for Boris and me. We grieved for months, and I miss him to this day. We lived, the dog and I, in his house, hunted his forest, visited his grave. When Boris died, I buried him beside his master, that neither might be alone.

It was impossible to stay there then. Only his affliction had forced Mischa to do that. I came out into the world again, a better man than I might have been. Educated. Understanding of suffering. Tender with children and animals. I love and suffer for the world.

But I have begun to wonder about my father. Sometimes in mid-winter I find myself beginning to have strange cravings. Hair has begun to grow between my fingers. I hunt no more, for the scent of blood intoxicates me.

Who—or what—was Peter Orlov?

Something like this actually happened in New England, several years ago. The news account I read triggered this tale.

OWL

I've lived here, man and boy, for nigh onto seventy years, heard every sound that comes out of the forest, seen near about every creature that lives there as well. The cabin where I was born is gone now—it was right inside the edge of the wood, and at night I used to feel as if the trees were leaning over it, whispering about how to get rid of us.

I live in a condominium now, but the complex stands where trees used to rear up so tall they seemed to scrape the stars. The forest has retreated beneath axes and chainsaws until it's now a mile away, and what there is seems a pitiful remnant to anybody who saw the real thing.

Most of us in this development are old. There's nothing much left here for young people to do, now the lumber is mostly cut, so they move to Portland or farther south. We in the complex grew up here, and we all know the woods in different ways. It makes for interesting tales in the cold Maine evenings, when a dozen or more of us sit in the cozy lodge parlor and swap lies.

Solomon Williams has bear stories. He was a hunter in his day, and he killed some and ran from more, and every one of them made a tale that keeps him supplied with listeners. Lattimore Reese has fish stories. Lord, does he have fish stories! Most sound like lies to me, but I was never a fisherman, so I can't say for sure. Luella Ryan was a plant specialist and used to wander the old forest looking for rare species and special herbs. She's a fine source of natural remedies, which is why so few of us go to the doctor much. That stuff tastes awful, but it does the job. We've got to be the most regular bunch of old duffers in the world.

I was a bird-watcher, when I could walk to do any good. My job running the lumber mill was hard, and in my spare time I used to head out through the woods, compass in my pocket, and walk for miles. There were always birds twittering away or cawing or making weird noises, whether you could see them or not.

I was never one to make a hard job out of fun, so I didn't carry books or binoculars or a notebook to write down what I noticed. I just sort of let everything wash over me and carry away any bad humor I'd brought away from the mill. I always liked the owls best. You didn't hear them in broad daylight, but if you got out really early or very late in the evening you could hear their eerie hoots from the deeps of the woods. They flew like ghosts, and when I was a boy I had a feeling they could carry me off, if they took a mind to.

Sometimes, even after I was grown, one would swish past me softly at head height, so close I could feel the brush of the air displaced by its silent wings. It made me feel strange, as if I'd come near something people had no business seeing at close quarters. I guess that's why this rogue owl gave me nightmares. The creature must have been displaced by the last work in the forest, when the government built a Forest Service complex in the middle of the old growth.

The first thing we noticed, back in early summer, was the lack of birds. That bothered me a lot, because as soon as it got warm enough to sit outside I kept an eye on everything that flew. When I went two whole days without seeing anything with wings except a jet, I got the others to start watching.

Luella was the one who realized the squirrels were gone too. Then her tomcat, Ruben, went missing as well. Anything that could handle Ruben had to be big and mean.

I knew Tom Benton, in charge of the Forest Service office, and I called him. "Something's going with the birds around here," I told him. "Not to mention other small creatures. Do you have any idea what it might be?"

Tom used to be a nice fellow, before he got to be a bureaucrat. Now he takes any such question as criticism of the Service. "We haven't done anything that might affect birds and animals," was the first thing he said. "You must be imagining it," was the second.

That made me mad. We may be old, here in the complex, but we're sharper than a lot of the young ones who are running things. We set up a watch, supplied with pads and pencils to make notes of anything unusual.

We counted birds, and in two weeks we saw three sparrows and a hawk, which was way up high. No squirrels. Not even the usual roving cats. When Mrs. Janifer's white Susie disappeared, we figured we were in trouble, because everybody in town knew that pussycat, and we all loved her. Not even the meanest kid in town would have hurt her.

It wasn't until Lucas Shannon, who lived in the big house at the end of Maple Avenue, went out walking his potbellied pig that we had ironclad proof that something unusual was happening. Lucas was odd. Some said crazy, but I maintain odd. I wouldn't want a pig for a pet, but there's no accounting for tastes, and when you have as much money as old Lucas does you can pretty well write your own ticket.

He had Porky Pig on a leash that morning. The animal trotted along just like a dog now, though training him had been a chore. I was on the other side of the street, crippling along on my walker, and we stopped to say good morning.

It was early, the sun just beginning to peep over the hill. While we called back and forth, a big shadow swooped along the street, not much more than porch-high, and grabbed that pig before Lucas could tighten his grip on the leash. Away it went, higher and higher, the leash trailing like the tail of a kite, until it was almost out of sight.

Then down came Porky Pig, kersplat, onto the street. Still alive, poor little creature. Lucas ran toward him, but before he could get there that shadow dropped onto the animal and spread its wings. Six foot wingspan, if it was an inch!

It was a great horned owl. Biggest I ever saw or heard tell of. Lucas backed off when it hissed, its eyes half closed and its wicked beak open. I swear the thing stood hip-high to the man, and Lucas is tall.

I was debating whether to stagger out and whack the thing with my walker when it took off, pig and all, toward the pitiful remnant of the forest. And that was the last anyone ever saw of Porky Pig. Lucas was really torn up about it, and I told him to call Tom and give him the straight story, so he'd know I wasn't just a doddery old coot with delusions.

He got Tom on the ball pretty fast. When the richest man in town chews your tail, you can feel the tooth marks for a long time, I suspect. Pretty soon here came Jimmy Butts in his Game Warden's truck, and we told our story. I could see he had his doubts, but Lucas told him to come back at twilight and see if he could catch a glimpse of that owl.

The day seemed to string out forever. By evening everyone in the complex was waiting to see if our monster owl would show again. Reese tried to get Lillian Trout to take her poodle for a walk, but she declined, much to his disappointment.

By sundown, Jimmy was there, his truck parked on the street, watching the fringe of trees toward the north. We were sitting on the sidewalk, watching from our chairs, when Luella let out a yip. "My God! There it is!"

"Where?" Jimmy got out of his truck and stared around, but by then the thing was right on us.

I had a minute of shock as the owl came at us. He was pretty far above my head, but Solomon was leaning on the back of Luella's white plastic chair. With a whisper of wind through feathers, the owl made a grab at his head and flew on, holding a small furry animal in his talons.

It was, of course, Sol's hairpiece.

Women shrieked, and men cursed. Sol was the loudest, but Jimmy Butts wasn't distracted by the noise. He reached inside his truck and came out with a shotgun in his hands. We all sort of sunk down in our chairs, and Sol crouched behind me with his arms over his head, though he hadn't any more hair for bait.

Maybe it was disappointed at what it found when it examined its catch. As twilight deepened, there came another silent rush down the street, and Jimmy upped with his shotgun as the creature came straight for him, as if it wanted to carry him, his truck, or both, away into the woods.

He blazed away, but that owl was fast. It banked around a huge oak in Shannon's front yard and was gone into the night.

* * * * * * *

After that life got to be exciting.

It was dangerous to go for an evening stroll that summer. Anyone who had a pet learned to keep it inside, except in the middle of the day. Over in the farming country east of us they lost several sheep, not carried away but so deeply cut by talons that they died. Lambs disappeared without a trace.

Jimmy Butts got to be a plain nuisance, he stayed so close. That shotgun must've rusted to his hand; he kept it with him constantly. But old Willie, as we named the owl, was wily. He never tried a frontal attack again.

When Jimmy was on Maple Street, Willie attacked a lady taking in wash on Garner, her cat at her heels. When Jimmy shifted to Garner, Willie turned his attention to Main and Chestnut, where he chased the Logan twins and their dachshund through their garden and into the house, scared out of their minds.

It got to be a regular duel of wits, in which poor Jimmy was outclassed all the way.

Nobody intended to risk a pet as bait, and as the only thing that attracted him was some small animal, we wondered if we'd stay in a state of siege until winter. Finally, Lucas Shannon came up with an idea, probably the only one he ever had in all his life. The fate of Porky Pig still rankled with him.

"I'm going over to Pinston and buy a lamb—or a goat, if that seems best, like they used to do hunting tigers. We'll stake it out, have Jimmy behind the bushes ready with the twelve-gauge, and get him in the act."

"I'm not going to be out in the open again," Solomon quavered. "I got me another hairpiece, but they're not cheap, and I don't intend to lose it or an eye or anything else off my anatomy. I'm going to be inside, with the door closed, no matter how hot it is."

Most agreed with him, so it turned out that Luella and I, sheltered under the big maple on our side of the street, were the only ones there to witness the Great Horned Owl Battle. I have to admit that I wore an old pith helmet I dug out of my closet, and Luella wore a sort of witch's hat she made of screen wire, but we had the guts to be there.

Jimmy was invisible. He'd rigged himself a sort of blind out of hedge clippings and hardware cloth. Looked just like a bush, he did. Once in a while I could see a glint of metal from his shotgun, but otherwise he was well concealed.

The twilight crept up, faster now that it was getting on toward August, and the goat tied to the parking meter gave a bleat. I never felt so sorry for anything in my life. This was none of its problem, after all. It was a little bitty goat, less than knee high, white as cotton. As it moved around the parking meter, I felt rather than heard soft wings flapping in the dimness.

Luella grabbed my arm. "Look!" she breathed into my ear.

The owl took a trial run, spotted the goat, turned somewhere out of sight, and came back low, its talons reaching, ready to grip. The shotgun deafened me and stray pellets spattered Luella and me both. There was a splop in the shrubbery beside us, and I heard the bird thrashing around.

I pulled myself up on my walker and started toward that poor goat.

"You all right?" Jimmy yelled.

"You sprinkled us a mite," I said. "Your bird's over in the lilac bush." I kept moving toward the goat, which was now twined so closely around the meter that he was about to choke.

Lucas came out of his house and looked over his gate.

"You can come on out," I told him. "The thing's either dead or soon will be." I was now beside the frantic goat. "You mind if I have your goat?"

He dawdled toward me, looking warily toward Jimmy, who was rustling around in the lilac bushes. "You want that thing?" he asked, staring down at the small white creature.

"If it can take such a risk for us, the least we can do is take it in and make it welcome," I snapped at him. "I've got a patch of garden behind my condo, plenty of room for such a bit of a thing. He may chew on the shrubbery, but what the heck—the shrubbery never did me any favors."

So that is how I met the biggest horned owl ever and got me a pet, in the bargain. Hero (good name, don't you think?) keeps me hopping. I'm walking without the walker these days, and Luella and I have decided that the two of us together make one pretty good old crock, so we've got engaged.

We go for walks in the woods, with Hero on a leash. We don't go at twilight nor yet at dawn. Where one owl of that size could live, another might be growing.

You don't get to be our ages by being damn fools.

Fantasy has elements of horror, particularly when the villain gets what he deserves.

BEHIND THE DARK PEAK

The sun set red. As its hazy ball touched the black peak across the valley, a gong sounded, echoing sullenly from the enclosing heights. Jerron sat on a rock and listened until the booming died away, but her eyes never left the eminence that was now silhouetted against the sunset.

Her hand clasped about the hilt of her blade. A frown creased her smooth brow, and her black eyes shone almost crimson in the fading light. Then the sun was gone, and the wooded ridge fell into dimness. The valley was now only a puddle of shadow, its farm-steads and walled fields invisible.

Jerron rose, and the lone watcher rose also, and came to her side. Though Jerron stood upon two feet and Erno upon four, they had much the same air about them, even in the twilight. Both were dark as to clothing and fur. Both were well-armed, Jerron with good steel and Erno with white fangs and curved claws.

"Now, if ever, we can cross to the peak, old friend," the woman said to the beast. She took up a small pack. With a hunter's stride, she found the faint path and moved toward the lip of the ridge. The yer-fox followed, as it had done for many months, and the two melted into the evening.

A giddy path switched down the steep. Bushes brushed against Jerron, and small stones rolled under her boots, forcing her to go slowly and carefully. It was well they did. As she paused to feel out the path ahead, her neck-hairs bristled. Behind, Erno breathed an almost-growl of warning.

Jerron felt her bones grow cold. More than once in this long quest she had found snares set in the way. The snares of wizards make those of hunters look kind by contrast. Some black web, she knew, was laid across the way.

"We have survived others," she whispered to Erno, but the words were for the comfort of her own spirit. The yer-fox knew no dread. Only its own loss and anger brought it at her heels in search of the sorcerer beyond the dark peak.

Now the beast sidled past on the narrow trail. With sure paws and superior vision, Erno took up the lead. Jerron sighed with relief. She knew that the mythic animal's senses were keener than her own, and would give warning of any peril long before any human traveler could identify their danger.

The beast did not forge far ahead of its companion. Jerron could feel the soft touch of its brushy tail against her knee as she crept after it. That told her the snare must be very near, and she drew forth her weapon with one hand and with the other the sacred relic that a priest had given her.

Slipping the bit of carven wood into her gauntlet, she set Imperator, her father's weapon, in her left hand, leaving the right free to cling to shrubs and saplings for support. For now the way had become even steeper, the stones more treacherous, and the feel of danger all but stifling.

Something touched her face. So deep was the darkness that she could see nothing, so she halted and set her feet solidly. "Erno?" she whispered into the blackness, and at once she felt a reassuring warmth against one knee.

The wisp touched her again, as if a trailing cobweb fluttered across the pathway, though there was no breeze and it was not the time of the year when cobwebs blew. The thing felt clammy, and Jerron crouched low and swung the blade above her head in an arc. There was a spark of green light threaded across the way and among the small trees, patterning the night with eerie brightness. Jerron shuddered. She had once seen a man caught in such a web, and the memory of that convulsed figure, glowing green, and the sharp stink of burnt flesh still made her skin creep.

"If I had been a chance wanderer, unwary, and had stepped through that first tendril, you would be alone, my friend," she said to Erno, who had cowered against her. "Yet Alloys knows that I will come, forewarned of many of his tricks and traps. Was that set for me, or for any who might come from the south?"

She went forward now with utmost caution. Where Alloys Light-Wielder had set one trap, he might well set more. Jerron had followed her lost sister, Licia, for months. She had met and survived other seekers after loved ones slain or abducted by the wizard.

Knowing that she was Licia's sole hope of escape from Alloys, she had guarded herself more carefully than had been her wont in her troubled life. Now she felt a certainty that she was drawing near to the place where Licia was held captive.

Erno's high voice sounded faintly at her heels. Not quite a yip. No, an eager sound, much like that the animal made when sighting game.

"You, too, feel that we are near?"

The yer-fox spoke again and pushed forward, as if to rush down the trail.

Jerron caught his brushy tail as the beast went past. "Slowly, slowly, Erno. There may be better-hidden secrets between this spot and the valley. You will find no vengeance for your sacrificed mate and her starved cubs if you fall into a snare and die within sight of your goal."

The yer-fox paused and pressed against the woman's leg. Jerron could feel the shudder that passed through its body. She had known for a long while that the animal understood her words.

The blade still glowed faintly green, and a dim throb of power came through the leather-wrapped hilt. She swung it ahead of her, as they eased down the trail, and now Erno stayed behind.

Faint light marked the sky above the adjacent heights, with trees bulking dark against the scanty scattering of stars. There was comfort in that, and Jerron moved a bit faster without realizing it. She stopped abruptly as a slender shape, regular and obviously artificial, caught her eye. One—she looked about—two—and a long scan of the surroundings brought numbers three and four into view. Columns stood, two to the right and two to the left, upon what must be a flat space in the pathway.

Her heart beat faster. Something dangerous lay between those innocent shapes. She knew it with a sense she had not known before beginning her quest. Taking the weapon firmly into her right hand, she thrust it between the first two columns.

There was a blaze of light. White and eye-searing, it illuminated the side of the ridge in all directions. She jerked Imperator backward and laid it on the path, for the hilt had grown too hot to hold. Its hot light pulsed on in the square formed between the pillars.

That grew in power, and Erno whimpered and ran back and forth, seeking a way around. There was none; beyond the outer pair, only emptiness loomed, a sheer drop of many yards.

Jerron turned her back on the display, letting her eyes rest from the glare. She pulled from her gauntlet the bit of carven wood. "It is not holy of itself," the priest had told her. "It is simply a focus. If your cause is good, if you are possessed of courage and faith, then it will send the thing that you need. But the impulse must come from you. If you are doubtful or guilty, you may find results you neither need nor want. Be warned, my child."

Now Jerron knew that she must trust to the honesty of her goal and the integrity of her heart. Many times she had almost resorted to the use of the relic, but always she had managed to avoid dissipating its virtue in a situation that could be handled in another way. Faced, now, with the urgent nearness of her goal and the perilous fires before her, she took the thing into her hand and closed her eyes.

Erno whimpered again, pressing against a knee, but Jerron was absorbed in her effort. She thought darkness. She summoned up the essence of all night, as the antithesis of the brightness that blocked her path. When she opened her eyes, there was a boil of smoky mist from the thing in her hand. It coiled and curled into the square between the columns, filling its space and pinching out the light. Bit by bit the brightness died away, until only the night reigned there.

Jerron thrust the blade of Imperator between the columns yet again. There was no spark of light. Even the green glow from the web was wiped away in the darkness there.

"This would have been the last," she told the yer-fox. "No one could have passed here who was not armed with other than mortal steel. The sorcerer would not think that I, a mere woman and witling, according to his assessment, would have known that she must have more than ordinary aid to combat his traps. Now we can hurry, for I feel the fields below are empty."

Erno leaped past and was gone. Jerron went after, and soon the pair found themselves upon a cart-track that wandered between hedges and walls. The warm scent of sleeping cattle breathed through the air, and the smell of fields came upon the light breeze that had sprung up from the east.

They went cautiously but quickly, knowing that even Alloys would not entrap the farmers and villagers who supported his demesne. Strangely, not a wakeful dog barked to mark their passing. Jerron wondered if there lingered, still, a trace of the power she had summoned into the relic in her gauntlet, concealing them from all they passed.

Still, she did not trust to that, taking a circuitous route to avoid clustered houses. Midnight found them beyond the settled part of the valley, partway up the slope of the peak looming above it. She had been told tales concerning the best way to approach Alloys's hold beyond the dark peak. Some had been laughable, some impossible, but a few had seemed to hold a bit of plausibility. Every one had spoken of a path that split from the main roadway to circle the shoulder of the peak. A dim way, to be sure, and hard to find even in broad day, but one that approached through a screen of timber and up a concealing gorge. She had determined to seek out that path, if it existed, and to try it. The alternative of going boldly in by the principal road, up to the high gates, and ringing their iron bell did not appeal to her at all.

Light would be required, if she were to find that pathway. She stopped in a level spot on the slope, concealed herself in a thicket of gorse, and waited for dawn. Erno sat beside her, huddled close for warmth, and the two dozed until first light touched the eastern sky. Then Jerron looked closely at the surrounding slopes, though she did not move from her place of concealment until she had located the faint trace that marked a trail.

"It goes in the proper direction," she said to Erno. "It leads toward the three leaning stones, as the tales said. Surely this must be the way we seek."

They moved, stooping, across the span of low growth to the hoof-trodden trail. Wild sheep, she could tell by the dung, used it regularly. There was no mark of a human foot. Before the sun rose, they had passed beyond the leaning stones and could see, lying in the shadow of the great peak, the broken lands beyond it.

As the sun moved higher, sidling over the height, it touched with light a massive building standing on an eminence rising beyond a rough valley, cut with gorges and ragged with trees. Their path led downward now, and soon they found themselves between stony banks set with boulders, walking beside a stream, still young but showing signs of growing powerful farther down its way.

The cut descended rapidly, but Jerron went with caution. Surely the sorcerer would know of this back-door entry to his hold. Even more surely, Alloys would have it guarded well.

They went away from the burgeoning day, again into night, as the walls of a gorge grew about them. In the distance, still downward, they could hear a mutter that grew to a roar and spoke of falls that gnashed against rock. The waters had nibbled their way through the land in a very devious manner, turning and twisting and angling. Rounding a breast of rock, Jerron found herself staring into a gulf where another stream joined that she had been following. Only a narrow ledge cut into sheer stone edged the cauldron into which they dropped with a deafening roar. The path led onto the ledge, which wound about the curve of the hole and went out of their sight around a buttress of fallen scree.

"Here, if anywhere, I would have set a guard, if I were Alloys," Jerron said, more to herself than to the yer-fox.

Yet it was the only path. She had no thought of going back and trying another way. She felt Licia nearby, and she knew that her sister, talented beyond any she knew who were not wizards, must feel her own presence even more strongly. She set her foot onto the ledge, noting with relief that it was supported below by the bulk of the cliff, being cut, at some remote time, by the waters below.

Erno went before, his lighter weight and surer step testing out the stability of the ledge. The thunder of the falls drowned out their footsteps; the mist boiling up from below made everything they touched slippery with wet. Sooner than Jerron would have guessed, they found themselves at the point where the path wound out of sight.

Erno moved from view. Jerron stepped carefully, rounding the sharp bend, and found herself looking up a long, narrow cut that, with the young sunlight shafting down against its westward wall, was not unlike a temple.

In the near foreground, athwart the path, stood an Ergerot. Its roars of anger at their disturbing presence had been masked by the falls, but now Jerron could hear every bellow, as well as the clank of the chain that secured it by the hind leg to an anchoring hasp set into stone. The big, hairy beast shook manlike fists at them, and she could see its four rows of serrated teeth, as it opened its mouth yet again.

Imperator came forth from the sheath, but Erno went more quickly still, straight for the throat of the creature. Its tiny eyes caught the light, as the yer-fox buried razor-sharp teeth in its furry throat.

Jerron groaned and hurried forward, knowing that the yer-fox had no chance against the larger, stronger beast. Yet she could not reach the creature's side or back with her blade, for the two were threshing about crazily. She looked aside and saw the hasp in the cliff-wall. Years of tugging seemed to have worn away the rock about it, and she set aside Imperator and brought her axe from the pack on her back.

With its broad base, she hammered at the rock, making chips fly and layers crumble. The tugs from the Ergerot helped, and she saw the hasp move in its fastening. Reversing the axe, she chopped viciously at the weathered stone. The hasp came free, and she turned to throw her weight against the bear-like beast.

"Over the ledge!" Jerron cried. "Let him go, Erno!"

The yer-fox strained the one eye that the woman could see in its socket, and in the dark glint of it she could see something like sorrow and something like triumph.

The Ergerot, focusing all attention upon the teeth in its throat, had not realized that it was no longer attached to the cliff. It leaned, tearing at the yer-fox. There was no chain to support it, and it fell into the gorge with a strangled cry.

Jerron leaned, shaking, against the rock. Erno was gone. She had not known how much the beast had eased the lonely hours and days and months of her search. Without looking over the edge, she spoke to the little animal. "I will do vengeance for you and your murdered mate, Erno. And for your cubs, dead before their time. I swear it." A tear touched her cheek, and she straightened and went forward up the gorge to the intersecting cut that she could see as a shadow ahead.

She came out into late afternoon. The path, continuing its unobtrusive way, led beneath huge trees strangled with mosses. The forest was scented with growing things, a healthful odor that seemed restful, even as she struggled onward. She reached the end of the path and the end of the day simultaneously with the end of her strength.

Dropping back into the shelter of the wood, she dug into her pack for dried meat and fruit. Her water bottle had been filled from the stream at the head of the gorge, and she broke her fast, drank deeply, and curled on her side, for she knew she must sleep before her final effort.

Jerron woke as the last star winked from view overhead. The walls of the hold were terribly near, for the wood ended just short of their bulk. The house itself was hidden, and she walked about the walls, looking for a place to enter.

The nether part of the wall reared up from a sheer drop. Time and weather had eroded the crumbling cliff side, leaving parts of the thick wall hanging partially over space. Animals had taken shelter beneath, enlarging holes into runs and tunnels. One such, Jerron found, led up into the kitchen garden of the hold.

She thrust her head up into a row of cabbages and looked about. No smoke rose from the many chimneys as yet, and even the kitchen-drudges had not begun their tasks. She pulled himself up, stood, and shook herself. Then she cleaned Imperator and hid her pack again among the cabbages. At the kitchen entry she tried the door and entered without hindrance.

It was a huge pile. Licia, she well knew, would not have cooperated enough to be housed well. It was more than probable that she was in a dungeon, if such there might be. Jerron searched quietly until she found an iron-bound door at the foot of a short stair. There she would begin her investigations.

A large lock was clasped through two hasps to secure the door, but the wood was old. Taking heed of her recent work with the hasp in the cliff, she dug away the doorframe and soon had the thing free, though its hinges squeaked dolefully. The steps beyond led downward, and she pulled the thing closed behind her and went down into blackness.

Feeling along the wall as she went, she found, at last, a torch-bracket, complete with torch. Her sigh of relief was heartfelt, and her flint-and-steel soon had a spark glowing in the oil-soaked tow. The light revealed another flight of steps, at right angles to the one upon which she stood.

There was no dust, and she knew the way was in use, though it might lead only to a wine-cellar.

At the foot of the last stair, she found herself in a long corridor, floored with flags and walled with cut stone. A metal-barred door barricaded the way, but she, no longer wary of noise, broke the lock with her axe. The echoes roused by the action ran crazily about the stone tunnels; in their wake came a babble of voices.

Iron doors lined the corridor beyond the doorway. With her axe, she hammered away locks as she went forward, asking each time, "Is Licia within?" Sometimes she had replies, sometimes only crazed laughter, and by the time she reached the bend in the tunnel, she was followed by some ten ragged scarecrows of both sexes and varying states of competence.

She found Licia chained against a wall in a huge, round room that held the trappings for torture. Her sister looked up, but the light hurt her eyes, and she hid them in the crook of her arm. Only when she spoke did Licia know who stood there, breaking her manacles. When she tried to rise, her legs failed her, but Jerron helped her to her feet and held her close, whispering reassuring words.

She should have known that Licia, weak and filthy or no, would need no such coddling. Once Jerron brought water and dried meat from the kitchens, the girl stood sturdily enough and turned her wan face to stare at her rescuer.

"Alloys wants to add my strength to his own," she gasped. "Strengthened so, he felt he might reach out to seize the power of the Great Wizard who advises the King. We have fought terrible battles, here in this place. I have not always fended him off, but he has not yet won. Tomorrow he might have conquered me, for it is the equinox of Fall, and his powers are augmented then. You knew that, I take it."

"I suspected, and so I hurried all I could," Jerron answered.

"But now," Licia continued, "he will find that matters have changed. You bear with you a thing of power. I feel it. Can you use it effectively?"

Jerron nodded. "With your help, I may be able to evoke even more power from it."

"Then let us go up. I know Alloys's chamber—he offered me its comforts, when I arrived. It disconcerted him when I refused them—and him."

The strange assemblage from the cells eddied about in the corridor for a moment after the two had made their way back to the tunnel. The darkness when the torch disappeared did not distress them, for many had known only night for years. Pulled by the attraction of motion, they followed at last, and came out into the hallway beyond the iron-studded door, just as Jerron and Licia were confronting a kitchen-maid in the corridor.

Jerron caught up the wench and bundled her aside into a wood-hole, securing the latch with a peg of wood. Then, followed by the freed prisoners, the two went up a broad stair, across a great, echoing hall and up another grand staircase.

At its top, Licia stopped at a double-leaved door upon whose surface was carved a bolt of lightning and a tongue of flame. Jerron broke the lock with her axe, and they entered the sitting-room, crossed it, and burst into a bed-chamber hung with silver and black.

"Alloys!" cried Jerron. "Wake, sorcerer! We have come to put an end to you!"

The undersized man in the great bed was sitting, already, his amber eyes sparking with fury. When he saw Licia, the fury grew to terrible wrath, and he flung himself from the bed, seized a staff, and shouted unrecognizable syllables into the morning air.

Jerron flung off her gauntlet and raised the relic between the two of them and the sorcerer. Touching Licia's shoulder with her free hand, she envisioned a barrier rising about and above them. Lightnings crackled and licked from the air, curling around the pair, but Jerron's hasty barrier held firm.

Licia closed her eyes, and a coil of mist reached out from the circle that enclosed them, snaking its way toward Alloys. He was wary, and a counter-spell dissolved the reaching tendril before it could find him.

Now the man was fully awake. Secure in ancient power, standing in his own place, he showed frightening confidence that he could destroy both intruders. Jerron could see regret in the bright eyes, as the sorcerer prepared to destroy the one he had needed so badly to consolidate his own abilities.

He drew a long breath. Jerron could see those amber eyes change color, becoming red—the red of madness. Something emanated from the night-clothed shape of the wizard—a vibration perhaps. Jerron felt her brain reel in her skull. Licia, beside her, stiffened, resisting. Then she fell against Jerron, who caught her, only to fall with her. Their shield winked out.

* * * * * * *

Alloys stood looking down at the two. Not the first, he thought. Probably not the last. He must strengthen his traps and defenses. Then the footsteps in the hallway caught the sorcerer's attention. He looked up to see a half-dozen wild-haired men and women shuffle through the bedroom door. He sent a blast of madness at them—but they were already mad, which was the reason they did not lie unconscious with their saner fellows.

One pair of eyes observed the wizard. "Alloys," said a cracked voice. Ten more eyes turned to him with interested attention. "Alloys!" they agreed.

He tried to run, but there was no other door. The window was beyond them. They caught him in a corner, and he did not come forth alive.

* * * * * * *

Jerron woke to deep quiet. She lay upon a parquet floor beside Licia, who was showing signs of waking. The sun was setting, its red light slanting through the windows onto the thing that lay in the corner, which did not need any more color, for blood stained it from head to foot.

Licia stirred and sat. She was whole, though worn past bearing by her trial. Jerron took her hand and lifted her to her feet. "Who?" she asked, gesturing toward the remains of the wizard.

"Not we," Licia answered. "Perhaps those he had most wronged. It is better so."

They went down to find the kitchens and to tend the freed captives, leaving Alloys Light-Wielder to stare blindly at the setting sun.

Sometimes I feel I have lived many lives in many different eras. This was not one of the pleasant ones! And that barrow still exists....

THE SLOT

Maeve crouched among the bracken, her ears straining. The lack of sound did not reassure her, for her hearing, along with her vision and her wits, had been waning for a long while. Desperately, she peered from her clouded eyes into the predawn dimness. Nothing moved about her but the chill wind of midwinter.

She licked her lips, her nerves singing with tension. So very many years had marked her wait for this moment that she was almost overcome with anticipation. Some among her kind said vengeance made a poor bedfellow, but Maeve had lived for so long with that as her sole reason for living, she had long ago forgotten gentler things.

The time was passing. Dawn was breaking, and no one was stirring. She stood cautiously among the winter-killed vegetation and shook out her skirt. It was painful to straighten her mutilated legs, but she persevered until they would serve her. She recalled sharply the night she had been crippled.

Red Osse had dragged her to his bed from her place among the maidens. Afterward, he had amused himself by cracking her bones and burning her flesh. Those external scars were the least of those she bore; those within her spirit still festered, though forty years had passed since they were burnt into her soul.

Now, at last, the priests had failed their trust. They had grown fat and lazy over the past decades, and on this most important day they had forgotten this was Midwinter Morning. They were not up and ready to put food into the side chamber of the barrow where Red Osse had lain moldering for ten long years. The ritual would not be performed for the continued well-being of the dead, as the sun shone its once-a-year beam through the slot into the tomb.

Better spirits than that of Osse would suffer because of this, she knew, but Maeve did not grieve for them. Every Midwinter Eve for the past ten years she had hidden in the dead bracken, watching and waiting for the thing that had at last occurred. Something inside her warped mind had known this time would come, that she would sooner or later be freed to work her will upon her tormentor.

Dawn light grew stronger. The day bade fair to be clear, no clouds touching the sky and only a little fog rolling among the hillocks around the great mound where Red Osse lay with generations of his family.

Limping wretchedly, Maeve made her way toward the structure, which rose abruptly, smooth and grassy in summer but now covered with winter-scalded turf. She scrambled and panted upward, glancing over her shoulder from time to time to gauge the sunrise. She felt that she was going to be in good time, for she had measured that distance often on her painful, stumping legs. She had rehearsed her actions over and over, so that now her journey up the mound seemed easy and quick.

She reached the top. There was the stone lintel, with the narrow slot let into the space between it and the slab above it. The sky was turning rose-colored in the east, and she knew Red Osse would be hungering, in his dark chamber, for the food and the chants, the rituals and the shaft of light that this one day of the year would bring to keep his spirit there among his people.

She saw a flicker of motion, far away toward the village. She frowned, trying to focus her fogged vision, but nothing would quite come clear. She shrugged. Whatever it might be, even if the laggard priests had recalled their duty, it would come too late. The sun was on the point of rising, and the next few minutes would see her years of waiting at an end.

She sank onto the stone, turning her back to the sunrise. With her face near the slot, she spoke. Her voice echoed eerily in the tomb.

"Osse, this day you will go into limbo. No light will reach your deep resting place. No food will come to you in time to hold your spirit here. The songs will be sung too late, and I, Maeve Ashworm, will hold the sun away from your eyes!

"You forgot me long before our son was born. When he died, you did not weep. You laughed at the crooked creature tending the cook fires, forgetting that you had made me so. If you remembered me at all, it was only as one night's cruel pleasure. Now you will remember me to your sorrow!"

She stretched herself painfully on the mound, forcing herself against the slot. Her withered breasts and lean belly pushed against the narrow opening, stopping out every hint of light. The sun's rays, warm against her back and her neck, warmed her shoulders through her thin shawl. Not a trace of its light could enter the tomb.

From far and deep, she heard a hollow sound. Was it a groan? She smiled with pleasure and pressed harder against the stone.

Now even her unreliable ears could hear the babble of sound from the village. Someone had, indeed, remembered. Someone had routed out the priests and the singers and those who carried the food, but it was all too late. She cackled aloud, her laughter ringing over the huge knoll of the knowe.

Beneath tons of stone and shale, turf and clay, layered with care and precision in the time long forgotten, there was another sound. Anguished, lost, full of fear.

Her body, that part pushed into the slot, felt a subtle change of pressure. Something struggled for breath down there, though nothing in the tomb had breathed for years. The pressure thrust at her body to the point of pain. It was no touch of hand or weapon, she knew. No, a force of will was set against her fragile skin and bones. She grinned, a spasm as much of pain as of joy, and resisted that force.

There came at last a crack of sound from deep inside the tomb. As the sun moved up past the lips of the slot, past her blocking shape, the sound ceased. All was silent now. She rolled over and looked up into the eyes of Dhuin, the chief of the priests.

Her smile taunted him, even as his staff crashed down upon her thin skull, spilling her brains onto the rock. Then he stared up at the sun, down at the tomb that had grown suddenly ominous.

Hungry, dissatisfied spirits must now fill the place. Those who had not been fed with light and food and ritual might still be soothed—yet that one, greatest of them all—what of Osse? If he still retained any of his strength, what might he not do to his unfaithful servants?

He shuddered. Gazing up at him, the lesser priests, the acolytes, and the attendant people of the village shuddered in their turn. Not one set his gaze upon the vast doorstone. Not one seemed eager (or even willing) to set a hand to open it.

Some dark passion lay over the place, and fear was a great part of it. Dhuin knew that none of his kind would ever dare to go inside the tomb again. The offerings that had been brought were useless. He gestured for them to be laid on the turf beside the doorstone.

The group milled back, as Dhuin descended to stand among them. No word was spoken to break the ominous silence. All turned together and hurried toward the village, leaving the old woman to stare in blind triumph at the defeated sun.

Sorcery can be a very horrible thing, when used wrongly.

A TOWER FOR THE SORCERER

Stoneheaver is dead.

It hardly seems possible. An hour ago he was booming orders to the carriers, directing the placement of the masonry and mixing the mortar. The wall was almost done, and he had been very pleased to have completed the work so much more quickly than the Prince had expected. His huge presence had filled the work-area with energy, even for the half-starved serfs who had been pressed into service for the Prince's project.

Between a great laugh at some quip from a carter and his next bellow of directions, he had stopped quite still, his hand against his chest. A look of sheerest astonishment had spread across his face. He made a little gesture with his other hand—the left—and I came to his side and caught him by the elbow.

"What troubles you, Master Stoneheaver? Are you ill?" I had hardly uttered the words when he toppled headlong, dragging me to my knees beside his now quiet body.

And he was dead. Simply as that. It fills me with fear. He was not yet in middle age. Hale and well every day of his life since I can remember. But the work must continue. God grant that I may be able to please my Prince in its completion.

* * * * * * *

Already I am being called Mason, as if this work had always been my own. It has, of course, been my only trade since I was apprenticed to the Master when I was a lad. Yet it was always his. It makes me feel strange to be trying to fill his big shoes.

The Prince was pleased with his ornamental wall, it is true. He called a stone-mason from his father's Court to check upon the work, after Stoneheaver's death, and that skilled personage could find no difference between the work done before and that done after. I had learned well from my Master. His wife is kind to me. I will care for her as if she were my own mother, do not doubt it. And Stoneheaver, from Purgatory, it may be, will be pleased with the things that I do.

But would he want that I should build a tower for the Sorcerer?

That one has an evil reputation. I have consulted with the priest, but he says that only the Bishop could absolve me from the duty to obey my Prince. And the Prince has taken this necromancer beneath his wing, so to speak. For political reasons, I have no doubt.

I know what the Bishop will say, for he is the Prince's uncle. So I must needs do as I am bid, whether I like it or no.

* * * * * * *

This is a strange thing that we are engaged in constructing. The base is huge. Ten yards across, it is circled by walls seven feet in thickness. Each stone must be set with much perfection, making a true curvature. Six serfs have been set to trim the interior of the wall, for the Sorcerer demands a smoothness that not even the King has ever seen.

He is much interested in the mixing of the mortar. When I deal with the bone-burners, he watches and listens. When I arrange for the killing of the pigs, that their blood may bind and strengthen the bonding of the stones, he looks with hooded eyes and secret smile upon the noisy deaths in the slaughter-yard.

I will not allow even him to watch as I mix the sand with the bone and the lime and the blood. It was Stoneheaver's secret, and I was sworn to reveal it to none but the mason who succeeds me. The Sorcerer misliked it, but he did not grumble overmuch. In some manner, that troubled me more than his shrieking rages.

* * * * * * *

The third tier of masonry is rising. This is a strange tower, indeed, its walls thicker than those of a Keep. As if it might be called upon to withstand assault. I have no liking for this task and will be more than glad when it is done and my obligation discharged.

The Sorcerer is most particular about this third tier of stone. This will be his own quarters and his working-room. He measures constantly, and we have torn out stones, more than once, that did not adhere to his prescribed measurements. He mutters, as we raise the stones, as we apply the mortar, as we finish each course. Spells, I do not doubt. It makes me quease to think of what he will do here, in this place that I have built for him.

I like even less the fact that he has insisted upon taking over the supervision of the bone-burning and the blood-taking. It is quieter, with the noisy slaughter pen removed into the forest. It is easier to breathe with the stench of the bone-smoke moved away to the river-edge. But I do not trust him to do these things properly. And why should he desire it? I have never before seen a nobleman who wished to dirty his hands with such things. It is not natural.

* * * * * * *

It galls me to make the admission, but the quality of the mortar is much improved since the Sorcerer began providing the ingredients. Only the clean sand that the carters bring from the distant sea is my own responsibility. The mortar is strangely smooth and easy to apply. It hardens to well-nigh impervious texture.

It is as well that the work is nearly done, for we lose serfs, day by day. They are running away into the forest, the foreman tells me. Frightened of the Sorcerer. Terrified by this Tower that is unlike any ever seen hereabouts. New ones must be dragged from the neighboring Lord's fields and taught the work, and that slows our progress somewhat.

I have begun to hate the smell of the mortar. In what way is it different? I cannot tell, but each day I go into the mixing shed with more reluctance. The stuff clings to my fingers, my clothing. It is almost enough to make one want to wash in water, merely to remove it from the skin. Changing clothing seems not to help overmuch.

* * * * * * *

Tomorrow will see the ending of this unwelcome task. The Tower rises above the tops of the nearer trees, bulging slightly in the middle of each tier. About the topmost course will be a girdle of cut stones, laid with much precision. They are not ornaments, for they cannot be seen from the ground. But the Sorcerer insists.

I have begun making ready for tomorrow. It is hard to wait to be done with this work—it has borne upon my mind and heart with much weight. The vats of blood are congealing already, though they have just been brought. The bone-meal is cooling in the baskets. I will prepare the vessel, washing it carefully.

* * * * * * *

I was interrupted by steps outside the shed where I worked. It was an annoyance, for I had no patience with my people, as I had had before. Conversation at this late hour when everyone was asleep would do nothing but irritate me. But it was the Sorcerer, and I could hardly turn him away, as I was not actually mixing the formula. He entered with his usual secret smile and looked about the shed.

"You are, I see, prepared for tomorrow's completion. Good. Good. The blood is here? And the bone? Excellent. I am, as you can see, quite excited. I cannot sleep tonight."

I stood waiting for him to indicate what I might do. And as I waited, I watched. He was, indeed, excited. For the first time since I had known him, there was color beneath his waxy skin. The thin lips curled ceaselessly into that smile, and his wrinkled eyelids crinkled above the washed-pale eyes. His hands were in his sleeves, crossed over his chest, as he approached me.

"It is time for the final ingredient. The prime, the indispensable ingredient. Your mortar is wonderful stuff, Master Mason. It will be even better if it contains...your blood!"

The dagger was in my heart before I knew that his hands were free of the robe. I felt my life slip away between my ribs with blood that he was catching in a bowl. And when I was totally detached from my body, I saw him lift it, slit its throat, and hold it over the vats, one by one, until each of them held some part of my life's blood.

He must have watched through a cranny as I mixed the mortar, for he did it faultlessly, on the next morning. And my well-trained apprentices oversaw the laying of the stones as well as I could have done myself. The Tower is completed, stark and strong in the forest.

We watch, those luckless serfs whose blood he had taken, whose bones he had burnt for his purposes, and I. He is at his devil's work now. The fields will wither. The Prince will come against him, but the Tower that was built at the Prince's word is far too strong to fall before the Prince's arm. We are helpless to injure our enemy or to help our Prince and our people.

Our blood cries to Heaven from the stones, but our souls are unshriven, unblessed in their final moments. Heaven does not hear, and even Satan can think of no better Hell than this.

My grandfather's farm was my family's favorite vacation site, when I was a child. There were a log cabin, two fish ponds, pine woods— and a well containing a wrinkled grin....

THE WELL THAT WHISPERED DARKNESS

My grandfather's farm was at the back of beyond, so far and deep in the East Texas woods that you literally couldn't get there from here without prior knowledge. I looked forward to our summer visits with a mixture of anticipation and dread, in just about equal parts.

We drove through miles and miles of thick pine woods, mixed with sweetgum and hickory and ash; the forest loomed on either hand like big black walls. At that time, the paper companies hadn't yet bought up all the forest and cut it down. The woods we traveled were virgin timber, just as the Indians had known it and the first settlers had seen it. The car seemed to buzz along the rutted road toward something huge and dark and primeval. I didn't have the words for it then, but I had the feelings, and I never forgot them.

Grampa and Gramma usually knew when we'd get there. I never figured it out. They had no phone, and they only went up to the main road for their mail about once a week. Yet they never failed to have a big meal on the table and the wood-burning cook stove, and all the beds would be freshly made. We'd drive up and honk, and Old Rock would come out from under the porch and start belling like the Hound of the Baskervilles. And there would be Grampa and Gramma, bustling down the steep plank steps, hugging and exclaiming and assigning suitcases to me and Uncle Jude.

There was always a kind of shock those first few minutes. The farm was pretty well cleared, but those woods leaned over its edges, making you feel that you might be in some kind of pit or well. It was always a relief to get the bags into the house, to feel those stout log walls close around and the roof shut out the leaf-edged sky. I've gone many places since those days and seen a lot of things in remote parts of the world. Never yet have I felt as totally removed from the rest of the planet as I did on Grampa Anson's farm.

We always ate first, whether it was meal time or not. A huge meal, with roast pork and wild turkey and big baked squash and pickles and preserves enough to burst a boy's pants. Then, every time, came the moment that supplied the dread that seasoned the trip.

"Don't you want to go down to the well and get us a bucket of water?" Gramma would ask me. The big cedar bucket smelled dark and watery and mysterious when she handed it to me, and I'd catch the bail and nod.

She never sent me to the well in the dark. Why then do I seem to recall visiting it, every time, in the blackest of nights? It was as if that well oozed darkness from its big round mouth.

You approached it down a crooked path that wandered through at least three hundred yards of Grampa's woodlot. Beside it stood a magnolia so tremendous that nobody I've ever described it to believes me. Hollow all the way up and broken off at the crown, it was big enough to camp inside. I'd often thought it might be fun to take a quilt down there and spend the night. If only it hadn't been so cheek-by-jowl with the well. I never in my life went near that well at night. Nothing could have dragged me there. At night.

I hated taking off the wooden cover. The curb stood chest-high to me then, and it took some doing to slip the cover aside in its grooves. Each sound I made echoed deep, deep. Things plopped into unseen water. Things slurped and gulped down there. I knew they were just pebbles and bits of stuff vibrated off the plank curbing, disturbed by my awkward maneuvering of the lid. But they sounded alive.

I can still see the wisp of dark stuff that always whiffed up from the well, once it was open. Like smoke or black mist. It never lingered, but it always made me swing the heavy bucket up, fasten it on the snap catch, and lower away madly.

I hated the sound of that bucket going down! Each bump against the damp and fungus-ridden planking made a separate growl or grunt. As if the whole depth to the water was filled with angry... somethings...that hated being disturbed.

And when the bucket hit the water, there came a chuckling slurp that made my small-boy skin crawl. I thanked the God I only vaguely acknowledged that I was too short to see into that gaping wound in the earth. I never looked into it, not even when I grew tall enough. Something told me that I'd see a wrinkled-water face down there, gulping down the cedar bucket and glaring up, wanting more.

The trip back was anticlimactic. Always. But nothing would have made me refuse the chore. It wasn't just the look that could come into Gramma's eyes when one of us disappointed her either. It was something inside that told me that this was as close as I was likely to get to one of the mysteries of the earth. The intuition of danger both troubled and invited me. Yet there was never anything—anything at all—that happened to give my feelings any solidity.

* * * * * * *

I shook myself as I sat behind the wheel of my modern car and laughed. Strange the things that visiting old haunts will bring back. I looked across the straggly cut-over growth that was all the timber companies had left of the Forest Primeval of my youth. The crooked dirt road I remembered was now an oil-top that had evidently been cut through the corners that it used to right-angle around. There was nothing at all left of the mysterious, back-to-the-beginning feeling I used to have on this road.

The track to Grampa's and Gramma's was still clearly marked by the two tremendous hickories that his own grandfather had planted on his grant. The cattle-guard was rickety, and my low-slung sports car rattled and shimmied going over the many-barred structure. Beyond, the double track was dim, overgrown with Bermuda grass and goatweeds.

The fields, even grown up with persimmon sprouts and sassafras, looked larger than I remembered, a strange reversal of the usual. Then I realized what made that. The forest that had leaned over on all sides was gone. The fields were wide open to the sky now, and it wasn't easy to find the point at which the straggly fence marked off the boundaries.

The house came into sight more quickly than in the old days. Much of the front part of the woodlot had been cut, leaving the square structure sagging in plain view. I pulled up into the front yard and looked at the stout house my childish eyes had loved. The roof was crumpled gently inward. The walls seemed, somehow, softer. It made me feel as if the whole building was quietly being dissolved back into the soil it had come from.

A big lank dog came from under the porch. Its half-blind eyes regarded me. A growl rose in its throat. Its hackles were up, and it looked as if it hadn't eaten in weeks. Since...Uncle Jude had died?

"Rock, good boy, Rock! Here boy. Take this!" I reached into the other side of the seat and pulled out the sandwich I had refuse to eat after paying far to much for it at a roadside eatery. He pounced on it as it hit the ground.

I got out very cautiously. He looked at me, gave a half-hearted growl, and sniffed. Then he wagged his tail. One twitch right, one left. I understood. He was very much like...his great-grandfather, the Rock of my childhood. I smelled like an Anson, so I was all right.

The porch was spongy underfoot. The steps lacked a couple of treads. Only my Gramma's scarlet climber rose looked healthy, and it had taken over the entire roof of the porch, dripping late blossoms and petals around its entire perimeter. The door had sagged to meet the floor. I pushed it enough to slip inside the parlor. It was dark, damp. The smell of mildew was all around me. Uncle Jude must have been too old and ill to care for things in a long time.

There was nothing in that house for me. It was full of death. The death of a house takes a lot longer than the death of a man or a generation of men. The house had died. I wouldn't rob its grave. I slid out and pulled the door shut behind me. The building would melt into the ground, I knew, in a few years. Fitting, in a way. I would keep the land, maybe hire a tenant farmer to work it.

I walked around the side of the house and saw that the woodlot still stood, almost untouched. Or perhaps saplings I had known had made the big trees I now saw. The notion struck me to walk down the crooked trail to the well. Maybe the big magnolia still stood. I'd get a photographer out to get a picture, if it did.

Hickory leaves were mellow underfoot. The smell of fall was in the wood. That best of forest smells, I'd always thought. Little scuttling things moved in the undergrowth. I smiled, remembering how I'd always pretended they were lurking Indians or cougars or grizzly bears.

Around the last bend there was the shape of the magnolia, still defying time. There was the curb of the well. Even those cypress planks had softened and sagged with the passage of years, I could see.

I walked to the well, pushed the cover aside with the usual doleful sounds. I smiled to myself, thinking how I had always refused to look into its depths. How deep was the thing? I wondered.

I bent to look. A gush of dark mist rose into my face. A sound. A soughing, whispering noise, like words almost. I stepped back and rubbed my eyes. A magnolia leaf fell from a bough some twenty feet above me. It was lacquer-green, healthy looking. It passed by me, as if aimed, into the open mouth of the well.

Drawn, almost against my will, I bent to look.

There was a quiet slurp. The light from the sky reflected in the rippled water below. For an instant, I saw two dark, whirlpool eyes staring back at me. A rippled grin spread from curb to curb. The voice I had always known lived down there whispered, drawing me forward, forward, to hear.

My head swam with vertigo. I felt my hands grip the edges of the curbing, holding me from falling. Tremendous words thundered through my mind, speaking to some part of me that wasn't hampered by their unfamiliar ring. A laugh, rising from the roots of the world, engulfed me in its tornadic vibrations. My hands loosed their grip, and I felt myself bending farther...farther into the well. Something inside me wanted to know the secrets of the deeps that had been promised. Something...hit me sharply on the head, bringing me to my senses.

I staggered back, sat hard on the ground. Another brittle, dark green leaf had fallen from the tree. It was caught in the collar of my jacket.

Breathing rapidly, I scrambled to my feet. With trembling hands, I re-covered the well. The path looked terribly long, very dark under the big trees. But I ran up it, feeling the darkness behind me in the well, whispering.

I knew that I'd never come back, look back, think back. Let my childhood rest by the well, guarded by the magnolia. There was no returning to a small boy's memories.

Especially when they were still alive.

ACKNOWLEDGMENTS

"The Mine" was first published in *Eulogy*, June, 1996.

"Down in the Dark" was first published in *The Horror Show*, Summer, 1987.

"Cage of the Heart" was first published in *Pirate Writings*, issue 7.

"The Gift" was first published electronically in *Speculative Fiction and Beyond*, 1996.

"Grimm's Way" was first published in *Nocturnal Classics*, 1993.

"The Orphan" was first published in *AUGURY*.

"The Well That Whispered Darkness" was first published in *The Horror Show*, 1984.

ABOUT THE AUTHOR

The author of sixty-two books, more than forty of them published commercially, **ARDATH MAYHAR** began her career in the early eighties with science fiction novels from Doubleday and TSR. Atheneum published several of her young adult and children's novels. Changing focus, she wrote westerns (as **Frank Cannon**) and mountain man novels (as **John Killdeer**), four prehistoric Indian books under her own name, and historical western *High Mountain Winter* under the byline **Frances Hurst**.

Recently she has been working with on-line publishers. *A Road of Stars* was her first original novel to appear in print-on-demand format. Many of her out-of-print titles are now available from e-publishers fictionwise.com and renebooks.com; many other novels are being published by the Borgo Press Imprint of Wildside Press and Amazon.com.

Now in her seventies, Mayhar was widowed in 1999, after forty-one years of marriage, and has four grown sons. She now works at home, writing short fiction and nonfiction, and doing book doctoring professionally. Her web pages can be found at:

w2.netdot.com/ardathm/ and
http://ofearna.us/ books/mayhar.html

www.ingramcontent.com/pod-product-compliance
Lightning Source LLC
Chambersburg PA
CBHW050742250626
47155CB00005B/1879